Dedicated to the readers

The Creatures' Realm

Salaha Kleb

This book is entirely a work of fiction. The names, locations, characters and incidents in this novel are the work of the author's imagination. Any resemblance to actual persons, whether dead or alive, locations or events is solely coincidental.

All rights reserved. No part of this book may be used for reproduction in any manner without the author's prior consent.

Copyright © Salaha Kleb 2015

Bibliografische Information der Deutschen Nationalbibliothek: Die Deutsche Nationalbibliothek verzeichnet diese Publikation in der Deutschen Nationalbibliografie; detaillierte bibliografische Daten sind im Internet über http://dnb.dnb.de abrufbar.

Published and Printed by BoD—Books on Demand, Norderstedt

ISBN: 978-3-7392-0798-8

Contents

Information for the reader	i
Prologue	1
Before	3
Beginning	4
Prepare	13
Prowl	28
Lurk	35
The unwary	38
Resolution	47
Mutual	56
Oddity	58
Fellowship	63
A brave Man	72
Happening	74
Alert	78
Wails	85
Tribulation	94
Janderas	106
Ordeal	114
The Bane of Assistance	125
Shoulder to shoulder	135
To Grief, Avenge, and Come together	137
Among your Kin	144
Strain and urge	148
Help	154
Feast	158
To Face the Truth	160
Love and hate	170
An Honest Promise	180
Awakening	183
Inquiry	190
Knaves	200
Seeking understanding	203
The Face behind the Mask	213
Allies	228
What was, is and will be	246
E 0.6	257
Glossary	260

INFORMATION FOR THE READER

I. This is a story of the time during the Eras Dawn of Arjovan, taking place in E0.7, three years after the discovery of the land in E0.10.

Eras from Dawn of Arjovan to Eronomus' birth

Dawn of Arjovan
The Creatures' Realm
Raise of Armora
Fellenveil
Rise of man
Harganos' sword
Garhos Jaro
Vengarth rage
Neerdos' perish
Ferja's death
Eronomus' birth

II. An asterisk (*) indicates that there is more information about that which it marks in the glossary.

III. The names in this story do not follow English pronunciation. To help you pronounce the names nevertheless the following information on speech sounds may serve as a guideline.

Vowels

a as in *car*
e as in *end*
j equal to *y*
u as in *you*
o (short) as in *not* / *nod* / *lot*
o (long after 'r') as in *so* / *nor* / *or*

Consonants

g as in *gizzard*
v as in *van*
h as in *house*

All life under the Sun is equal—and to be treated with courtesy

Anonymous

Prologue

There! A truly imposing man—with strong arms and broad shoulders, bearing a keen blade and a bow—is striding across a glade, in a whisper saying, "Whoever you are, death shall claim you for your doings. All you have taken already, another soul and another soul and another soul. No more! I will find you and blame no beast for your doings—you cannot deceive me!"

With drawn blade he steps into the forest, heading for where many souls have gone missing.

"A cave," says he, recalling everything his kin have apprised him of: 'Not far from a prairie in the south is a cave, and there we found the body of a man, cut down with a sharp blade. We buried him in a glade through which runs a river, but long we may think: Whoever his slayer, he must be found—something foul is going on. People lose their way, end up adrift, are claimed by beast' or die of hunger; but this man, he has been cut down.'

Afore twilight he can see the grassland arising between the trunks of all the trees shading the earth; unfortunately, dense green foliage either blurs or obscures everything around him: long it may take to find the cave within this verdure; and for night will be descending soon—and hence preventing a search—, he proceeds straight towards the open field to camp beyond the forest's edge.

Yet, beside the largest tree he has ever seen in his life, with roots much taller than him, he happens on an abandoned wagon, with someone's possessions lying scattered about the rear.

For one wheel is broken and an axis as well, he imagines the wagon struck against a root or rock.

Whatever the cause of the crash, it may be that the wagoner traveled on by horseback along whomever else with him; though if so, "Why, then, did everyone leave his possessions?" he can only wonder.

Whilst drawing nigher unto the wagon, he stumbles across a blood-soaked body cloaked in lush greenery: a woman, barely in her thirties, cut down with a sword. However sad the site, it seems, he is close to finding whom he hunts; for whatever befell this poor maiden, there are traces of a fight, undoubtedly between two men by the size of the footprints—perchance someone struggled with her attacker.

A mere step away from the corpse a trail of blood shows on the foliage, leading him farther and farther into the forest at the onset of night.

Cleaving his way through the plant life, he comes to a halt on espying another body 'neath a tree; and there, just a few steps farther ahead, a figure is lurking about a shrub, a figure with gory skin and filthy hair: a whiff of menace is about this man, for he is holding a bloody blade.

"Foul man that you are," cries he. "Turn to face me!"

And the figure turns around, unveiling a familiar face. And the man can't but step back a pace, shaking his head, raising his sword, uttering, "Surjes!"

Before
Of a journal

There where I stood among trees and flowers in my search for game I awoke to the beauty of the realm I wandered, and yet death seemed to be hovering above me the deeper I dared to go.

In the gloom of night, when all I held was a torch, it came to me, emerging from the greenery around me; and I could see its gaping maw when the beast drew nearer, growling and trembling me to my very core. I could do nothing; rooted to the ground, I dared not to move, to breathe, to take but a step. That it would be quicker than me, that I knew; that it was stronger than me, by far more powerful than I could ever be, that I knew; that it was alone, that I assumed; that it would leave, that I would have never thought, but it did: though gnashing its teeth, striking the earth with paws broader than my skull, it did withdraw into the night.

I felt blessed, protected by a force beyond my understanding, virtually unable to grasp what being there stood behind me, scaring off all the critters near me.

Only just I could escape, running to the end of my breath through the dark 'til there came a glade where was the hill that I ascended to my future. Upon this hill I made a firm decision. Yes. I deciding to take up a demanding task, which might claim my life if ever I would forget the realm I live in.

Beginning
They found rivers and lakes, the greatest trees yet to be, and mountains of phenomenal height, and they came upon falls and glades in forests and wandered across plains covering a sheer endless range — it seemed everlasting.

For eons, from the very first era before the birth of Man to all the ages and centuries thereon, had the region endured, growing in greatness year by year. Ere the long-lasting stage of gloom and ash following frequent eruptions of volcanos, Mother Earth was flourishing at its greatest, yet thereafter, when darkness perished at sunrise and rain flooded the region, its foremost creations were born. Prime critters roamed the land and trees formed forests, which shaded the earth and brought forth new plants and flowers, which dispersed their seeds and sent their bloom past the trees, winded to and beyond plains, glades and more.

Long after the human race came to be, kingdoms began to rise only ever around this imposing region, for therein live beasts no men is due to tame. Yet, in E0.10, traveling tribes ventured unintentionally into this land in quest of their own grounds; and there, where no kings have ever been throned, ancient glories awaited them. It was unruled, unblemished and pure. Hence they claim the land theirs and named it after the word for (the) Sun in ancient tongue, Arjovan.

In the following year, they began to invite those who lived in oppression to join them and told all who had but little to call their own to come to them; and always, every day at dawn, they praised these sacred grounds that they had claimed their own, though remained blind of the beasts they were among. Many of these great critters are nocturnal and too strong to fight off, and they are by far too many to drive off. Living below or upon earth, roaming the land in packs or alone, hunting, fighting, scavenging, these creatures grew with the region; yet all that people had chosen to see was the purity of nature, the chance to begin afresh, to live where no sovereign could reach, and thus their efforts to be sheltered from the night's mortal threats have been a trifle. Above all else, villages were raised without a stockade or any other kind of barrier. Some of these villages are found in the forest, right within *the creatures' realm**, and though it is that inhuman cries make known whose place on Earth Arjovan is and how little can be done against something which sheer voice can deafen a man, people assume to be safe as along as they stay inside their houses or near a fire until dawn as it is this that had averted an attack by creatures in other lands before. If it weren't for a hunter who wanders from village to village to tell everyone that at night man-eaters wake to feed and that these beasts struggle not with a simply wooden door, nobody would be aware—actually aware—of the peril they have been in to this day.

    The hunter, truly an honorable and brave man, faced many dangers on his travels yet never lost his motivation or drive, and with his bow on his back and his knife in hand he heads through the forest, resting on trees at night and heading on at *day's first light**.

    The Sun's light brightens earth and sky when he comes across a small village in the forest, Odas. He halts in his tracks and roams the village with his eyes, seeing merely a few houses standing widely separated from each other. Plainly constructed homes which front doors cannot keep a man-eater from entering are everywhere dominating the village's appearance. That the people dwelling here survived until now is thanks to a fool's luck.

Men and women—some old, some young, others small or tall—are found outside, going about their daily chores. He sees them talking with each other, simply enjoying the life they share with one another, and it strikes him that they give little thought to the quickness with that it can end. What worries him even more than their thoughtlessness is that nobody seems to be interested in talking to him: they tolerate his sudden emergence as if he were one of them. In many ways this appears as if Odas has no Elder who's to decide whether he, a stranger who might as well be a scoundrel, is welcome.

Wondering whom he shall approach, he walks over to an old man sitting on a bench in front of a house and asks him who the head of Odas is. Unfortunately, he was right: the people living here see no sense in choosing an Elder and consider a show of hands better that having just someone telling them what to do. When there is nobody he can turn to, then the hunter must warn each and every soul personally—a truly time consuming task for someone who is in a rush as there are many villages more yet to be warned.

With annoyance he looks at the old man, understanding from his age that he has not much time left.

"May I ask you something more?" he inquires on sitting down next to the old fellow.

"You may."

"What is your name?"

"Is that what you wish to inquire of me, stranger?"

"I merely wish to know with whom I am speaking."

"Tarion is my name, and who is asking me for my name?"

"Artias."

"Well then, Artias, what did you wish to ask me?"

"I wonder, Tarion, I wonder if there is someone you can turn to when you're in trouble?"

"Well, I guess that be Arianna. But tell me, stranger, are you in trouble?"

"No, no, I merely wish to speak to her."

"About?"

"About the wilds, Tarion, about the wilds — can you tell me where I can find her?"

"Come, Artias, a walk will do me good."

Tarion rises and paces away as Artias asks, "Walk where?"

"To Arianna of course."

With a limp Tarion walks along a grassy path through Odas, glimpsing at Artias from time to time. A man of such height is rare and one of such supreme strengths as revealed by large arms and broad shoulders even more. Seeing Artias' strong legs, Tarion smiles.

"I used to walk a lot," says he, "but not anymore since I broke a leg."

"Were you a hunter?"

"A hunter? How come you assume so?"

"If I would be living in a village, I could not imagine any other reason for walking if it weren't for hunting."

"So hunting is where you heart lies?"

"Yes indeed."

7

Tarion escorts him away from the village to a house almost entirely surrounded by massive trees. There is merely a small track leading from Odas to the house, a track that has been used many times over as the flattened grass shows.

Embraced by trees near and far, they walk close by each other towards the entrance. To then discover that the front door was breached takes Artias aback, and he forthwith draws his knife while carefully treading closer, advising Tarion to stay behind him in a whisper. Quickly but carefully they enter the house, finding themselves surrounded by shards of wood. The door was opened with such force that the hinges were torn off the wall and the hooks securing the broken batten bent out of shape.

The house is small, barely larger than a hut and as roughly constructed, offering just about enough room as needed for a fireplace, two beds, a shelf, and a closet. Within quite the distance from Odas, with no solid fencing, this place is like a calling to every beast searching for fare.

"It just came in," they hear a trembling voice saying and thereupon see Arianna sitting in a corner, her arms embracing the body of a boy. "My boy, it killed my boy."

Her lovely eyes are drenched in tears, and she cries as she lays her head on her son's chest, wishing he'd still be breathing.

Artias crouches down before her, laying his hand on her shoulder. He can see the pain she goes through when she lifts her head and looks at him, gulping back her tears.

"We shall bury him," he says with a soft voice. "Come, let me help you rise."

He looks at Tarion and tells him to summon ever member of the village at once. "I have something to say."

Tarion nods and helps him carry the boy's body outside where they lay him down upon the ground, and then he departs to gather everyone.

"Do you have a shovel?" Artias asks Arianna.

"I told him not to check, but he would not listen — he simply went."

"Went where?"

"We heard a yelp and then there was a sound of scratching. I thought it's just someone trying to scare us, but it wasn't. He approached the front door and then something just forced its way inside and bit him in the shoulder. It sucked his blood. I heard how it was sucking. I tried to help him, but my efforts, they were in vain. It ran off when I came at it with fire, but my efforts were in vain — my boy, dead he is."

"How did that creature look?"

"Odd, bizarre! Yes, bizarre is the right word. Odd, so bizarre, with horns." She falls on her knees next to her son's body and holds him in her arms, crying.

"How could I let you go," she weeps, "oh, how could I!"

"You did not know what was out there on the prowl. Do not blame yo—"

"I did not know. I did not know, and now he is dead, because I did not know. I should have known ... I—"

"Tell me, Arianna, tell me how the noise sounded like?" Artias bends down and tenderly lays his hand on her back, stating that he must know. "It is of utter importance."

She does not hear him, though. Artias is quick enough to understand that the pain she feels for her son's death is so great that his words go unheard; and he thereupon, in utter silence, assumes in sight of her boy's color of skin that she is not his mother and perhaps took him as her child in hopes of giving him a better life, and though she might have given him just that, she feels as if she brought by his death.

It takes time until her tears are shed, and she withdraws from the body and lies down on the ground, staring at nothing but the tree crowns above. Lowering his head, Artias wishes he would have arrived earlier. Perhaps he could have saved the boy's life then. To show Arianna his sympathy is the only thing he can think of doing right now.

"In dead you will be reunited again," says he and continues: "And then you will laugh and smile and feel only joy." All that he says seems to fade away before even reaching her.

With struggle he leaves her alone to look around the house. He searches for traces, tracks, trails, or any other kind of marks that might help him find out what kind of creature assailed the boy. There is a track, much different to the one leading to Odas, coming from the forest. Whatever worn a path into the ground was heavy and had feet similar to such of a badger. Till to the house the track leads, and the wall emerges with scratches where it ends, deep scratches made by claws. The wall bears many such scratch marks some of which were made at the same spot, as if the creature had been trying to cleave its way in through the wall for a while.

Men and women come running to the house alongside of Tarion and gather around Arianna while others begin to look around the house in search of whatever it was that caused her son's death. Artias hears men taking to each other and trying to guess "what monster could have done such a thing to a young boy" as he heads around the corner, walking right into them.

"Halt," they say and seize him by the arm. "Who are you?"

"Calm yourself. I am here to help."

"Says you!"

"Ask Tarion. Now, let go of my arm, and let us return to Arianna together!"

"You know her?"

Artias gnashes his teeth and advises the men to let him go.

"I am here to help I said. Do not make it hard for me to do so."

"We shall ask Tarion whether or not he knows you, and then, then we will let off you."

They escort Artias to the others, as yet not knowing who he is. They ask their fellows who are helping Arianna on her feet if she is okay before they even think about seeking Tarion.

"She is not well," Artias says, needing merely a glimpse to tell that she never will be again. "As I see it, her son was attacked by something that had laid eyes on him and her for some time."

"What you mean by 'laid eyes on him and her'?" asks a man. "Who are you anyway?"

"His name's Artias," Tarion answers. "He is a hunter."

The man — not tall nor hefty but short and slim, with skinny arms and legs — approaches Artias, at once asking, "What did you mean by saying it had laid eyes upon him and her?"

"The wilds are full of dangers, full of creatures prowling about and picking their prey with caution. Whatever took the boy's life was feeding off blood." Looking at the guys on his side in whose grasp he is kept from moving, he tells them to let him go; and as they do so, he continues: "I do not know of any creature gulping blood, but whatever it was, it could come back. We must return to the village at once and bury the boy. We will see further from there."

All that the people hear is that Artias said it might return, and this rises fear in them, and they ask each other what can be done against such a peril.

"Tarion," Artias calls the old fellow to him. "Odas is near but she lives here. Why so?"

"Is that important!"

"To me it is."

"Well, I asked her many times to come to Odas, but she always said she rather live here. Her father built the house long ago. That is why she still lives here. That and because she says certain herbs grow not far away from her house."

"Herbs?"

"Yes. She, she treats the wounded and the ill as best as she can with these."

"So she is a healer?"

"I guess you could say it like that."

Prepare
There came a man who vowed that no soul shall be left to his death forth on. Pledged to protect he did, but as yet he knew not what would befall.

The folk of Odas begin to prepare the boy's grave at the rear of the village. Arianna is watching her fellow citizens digging a hole, with struggle trying not to think of the terrifying thing she saw and how it came bashing in, seizing and biting her beloved son—a truly dreadful incident.

AT THE HEART OF ODAS: Artias is talking with three men, who claim themselves hunters like him, to find a way to deal with the great critter, which could return again to feed once more.

With courage he stands before them as he says, "We could spend the night in Arianna's house and see what may come to greet us, but—"

"Are you mad!" one of the men says. He carries not only a bow but also a small axe and emerges physically strong. Having such a man's support in the coming night would certainly make things easier and less dangerous, yet Ardegan, as this man's name is, does not think Artias' idea a smart one; because "If something happens here in Odas, we'll not be knowing of it. When Arianna was attacked, nobody heard anything, so there is no telling if we will hear anything should our fellows be attacked tonight."

"Which is why I go alone."

"Alone? No! What man would I be if I'd allow that. I shall join you. My fellows will stay here and watch over Odas as closely as I shall over you!"

"Two men are not enough to guard everybody. We must find a way they can alert us. Say, do you have a bell?"

"No, I do not."

"Do you know someone who might have one?"

"Nobody in Odas has or ever possessed a bell. But I have a trumpet."

Artias smiles his joy and grabs Ardegan's shoulders with both hands.

"Splendid news! A trumpet, better even than a bell. I suppose your friends know what to do with it?"

"Blow it when they see something?"

"Yes, right. Now, I see so many ways into this village." Artias turns to the other two men on his side. Both of them are hearty and swift on their feet. Appearing capable of defending themselves and experienced in hunting, these two men are reliable assets. Tindras and Gilgaron, men with courage and strengths, willing to assist Artias in his cause, look keen to act.

"Let me ask you," says he to them, "let me ask you if your ears are sharp and your eyesight keen?"

"Do not worry. If something comes, we won't be missing it," say they.

Artias nods proudly and claps Ardegan on the back.

"Are you sure you wish to spend the night with me in a house I cannot doubt to be sought by the beast again?"

"I am."

"Very well."

"What about everyone else," Gilgaron asks with worries.

"I must know which house is built best. For that we must take a look at each."

"No need to," Tindras utters proudly. "I know which is best. Mine."

"I hope you do not mind having guests."

"Yes, well, Odas might be small, but I don't have enough space for everyone."

"I am aware of that. The houses are rather small indeed. Children and women shall be brought into your house. The rest—"

"They will be needing someone who can defend them should it come to an encounter."

"Whoever's good with the sword and not a coward shall stay with them, preferably four men."

"Not one of us knows how to wield a sword, Artias—we aren't warriors."

"I see." Artias reconsiders his plan quickly, looking around Odas while doing so. "Okay, let's do this differently, then. Is there a tavern in Odas?"

"Yes."

"Does it have two floors?"

"Yes."

"Show me."

The tavern—not a shabby nor moldering one but a simple and fine one built with effort and skill—lies not far from the track leading to Arianna's house and has, what is most favorable to Artias and his fellows, a balcony from where Odas can be observed better than anywhere.

"Everybody shall seek shelter in the tavern," says Artias. "They shall stay on the second story for the night and remain silent 'til dawn. Gilgaron, you and Tindras shall gather everyone and take them here, and all through the night you shall stay on the balcony and keep your eyes and ears sharp and your bows set. If you see something, then do not blow the trumpet. The risk that you attract attention is too high, so do only use it if you are in danger."

At Ardegan Artias looks when he asks him to get the trumpet, and then he lets all of his fellows know that he must leave them alone for now.

"I will seek you out later," he assures them.

"What are you up to?" asks Gilgaron. "You should not go to Arianna's house alone! I insist that we—"

"I merely wish to speak to Arianna, my fellow."

"If it is the beast you are going to talk to her about, then you should wait until she is herself again."

Artias knows this already and therefore waits until Arianna's son lies buried underground before he approaches her, keen on gathering as much information on the creature as possible. It is not easy to asks her about the very thing that killed her son, and he hesitates when she turns away from her beloved's grave, staring at him as if joy would never again find into her heart. And he—who cares for every soul he is among, striving to ward them and fight for them and even die for them—can see the tears by which her eyes shine and the few running down her cheeks. She may try to keep her feelings at bay when all that she desire is to scream, but O how great must be her pain, how unending her suffering.

"I wish I wouldn't need to ask you this," says he, "but I must for everyone else's safety."

"You want to know about the beast, don't you?"

"Yes."

She nods and draws a breath, looking back at her son's grave one last time before asking the hunter to join her on a walk through Odas.

"It was skinny, very skinny for its power," she tells him, treading the path with shaking hands.

"Could the ribs be seen?"

"What? Why would that matter? Are you even listening to me!"

"Arianna, I know of a creature that is slim but very powerful—"

"It wasn't slim. I said it was skinny, its waist was. It had no shoulders only such an enormous neck, and I saw horns across its skull."

"Horns you say."

"Yes."

Silently Artias thinks about all the beasts he has been dealing with to this day; sadly, not one matches her description: a creature with a skinny waist, a great neck, and a horned skull is nothing he has caught sight of yet.

"Tell me, how did its eyes look: big, small, sunken into the skull, or standing out?"

"Its eyes were green, yes, I remember. Green. But it is ... I do not know—please, it is hard for me to think of it."

"I understand," Artias says, aware of the torment he puts her through. "I shall not trouble you with this any further. Please, go to the tavern shortly before day's last li—"

"The tavern? Just why would I go there?"

He does not know whether it is wise to tell her of his worries; yet, sooner or later, she could find out about his secrecy, in which case she is not going to trust him anymore. Only the truth and nothing but the truth he decides to speak.

"It may return again for prey."

"I say, what can be done? If it comes, then—"

Before Arianna breaks down he says that he has slain many beasts already (which is a lie) and that he will protect Odas and her come what may. "Not a soul shall be taken by the beast anymore."

Looking upon the hunter as a strong warrior, she nods and makes her way to the tavern, preferring to be there before the Sun even begins to fall.

"I will not be seen outside any longer," says she, "no more."

"I do wish you only the best," Artias whispers and moves on in search of his fellows.

Ere long he finds his three allies near a house next to an enormous trunk of a great tree. Gilgaron's home comes in sight tiny next to the tree, although it is among the biggest houses in Odas, with a strong door—much unlike such of the others—and a porch.

"Have you fetched the trumpet yet," asks Artias.

"Yes," Ardegan says, showing him a trumpet in quite 'displeasing' condition—not quite what Artias has been expecting.

"Does it even work?" asks he, certain that it will sound just as it looks.

"Sure it works. You wanna hear?"

"No, I rather not have any creature hearing its sound until we will be needing it. I must ask again: Are you sure—and I mean absolutely sure—that it works?"

"I am."

"Good."

Nodding at the house, Artias says that he would like to discuss the steps to be taken in the coming night inside. Gilgaron does not mind having guests and even tells the hunter that he may come and go as he pleases. A kind offer but one Artias cannot accept, for it is not his home but his fellow's.

The front door appears solid; and inside, the house lets anyone who enters be filled with a feeling of comfort and warmth. The fireplace—truly nice and well-made, with a fine bench and table before it—adds much to the comfort given by four walls and a roof. Together they head into the kitchen and take place at a small table in the center, politely declining their host's hospitality.

"We have urgent matters to discuss," says Ardegan shortly, "so sit down, Gilgaron, and let us begin."

"Nightfall is approaching," Artias speaks loud and clear, letting no word go unheard, "and when all that lies around us will be cloaked in darkness, we must be ready to face death; so tell me, do tell me, my fellows, do you waver in sight of death?"

"We have never faced death before," say his fellows, "but we shall not waver."

"Fine men you are, strong and courageous. Let us go through—"

"Do you think it will come to the tavern?" Gilgaron asks.

"I cannot say it won't. Hopefully, though, it will come to Arianna's house, where me and Ardegan will be awaiting its coming—we will find the being in the dark."

"Maybe, maybe it isn't alone," Tindras utters anxiously. "We might be outnumbered here."

"I found a track leading from Arianna's house into the forest. It appears as if made by only one beast, not two nor three but one. Be that as it may, we cannot ban such a though from our thinking—it is always better to expect the best yet be prepared for the worst."

"I have been expecting the worst ever since I had seen her son's body—I knew him ... a good boy he was."

"I am sure he was. Now, you do still remember all that I have told you earlier I presume?"

"Yes." Ardegan speaks for the others.

"Each one of you does?"

"Yes." Tindras speaks for the others.

"Good. May you tell me again, then?"

"Whereas you and Ardegan will stay in Arianna's house for the night," says Tindras, "we are going to do so in the tavern and keep an eye over Odas. Should the critter show, then we shall only sound the trumpet if in danger—certainly, we must keep folks calm, too."

"So it is. Good, now, how well is your aim, my fellows?"

"I can pierce you a leaf, Artias," Gilgaron says, proud of his aim.

"So can I," Ardegan says, nodding to each word he utters. "No problem doing so."

Also Tindras seems confident. They are all skilled in archery as it seems. However, something leaves Artias' and Ardegan's fellows with bated breath, and they ask, "What if you will be attacked? You have no trumpet."

"We won't be needing one." Artias rises from his chair and draws his knife at once. "With this fine blade I shall cut its throat should it dare and face me."

"Brave words," utters Ardegan, "if you are going to keep them."

"Most certainly I will."

"I do not doubt so," says Gilgaron, "but do not act rash when under attack."

"I may be reckless at times but do not ever act foolishly, my friends."

"And how shall we take the beast down?" wonders Tindras.

"We need spears, or any long staff or stick with a pointed end."

"Staffs usually do not have a pointed tip," Ardegan explains shortly, "and neither do sticks."

"We will make them have one. We cut them to shape and hold the tips into the fire to make'm strong."

"So now all we need are staffs," Tindras says, "or sticks."

"So it is, my fellow. Do you have any sticks or staffs?"

"How long must they be?"

"Around eight feet (2.4 meters)."

"The forest has plenty," Ardegan comments.

"I am aware of that. I was merely hoping you might have one or two."

"Sorry," say his fellows.

"That's okay."

Artias sheathes his knife again and nods at the entrance.

"I will get us some sticks, and you, my hearty fellows, you should inform the people of our plan meanwhile."

"No," Ardegan cannot allow the hunter to go out alone into the forest, "I will join you."

"No need to—I am quicker on my own."

At a swift pace Artias leaves the house, allowing his fellows no time to raise objections. He strides straight into the wilds and begins his search near Arianna's house in hopes of finding something of interest such as another track. Though he finds quite a few sticks that will serve him and his companions well once cut to shape, there is no track near and far equal to the one he found earlier.

Standing in the forest all by himself (embraced by trees, barely able to see Odas through the dense vegetation), Artias looks up at the tree crowns, trying to catch a glimpse of the sky.

"I wish I were a bird," says he; "how much easier could I have traveled then, and perhaps I would have been quick enough to reach you in time. Your son, yes, his death is tragic, but what I dare not say to you … this realm is not ours but that of beast'."

Notwithstanding his belief, he shows his respect to Arianna's son by pledging to himself that nobody shall die tonight and that he shall protect the people of Odas, and then, to make sure that he really did not miss any tracks, he checks the ground one last time and thereupon returns with seven sticks upon his shoulder. They are heavy and make him sweat and swear at their weight until he can dump them in front of Gilgaron's home and stretch his back. Keen on having everything prepared as quickly as possible, he immediately looks around for his fellows, who are still going about informing everyone of the course of actions in the evening.

He draws his knife and sets about tapering the sticks when Tindras comes to him.

"You certainly were quick, Artias," says he.

"I know where to look—did you tell everyone yet?"

"No. I saw you was returning, so I thought I lend you a helping hand."

"Do you know were Gilgaron is? I should like to use his fireplace."

Because Tindras is a good friend of Gilgaron, he may enter his fellow's house at any time, needing no permission to do so, and this he tells Artias who cannot tolerate such a behavior. No matter how close they are, Tindras should ask his friend first before simply stepping into his house or use his belongings.

"Your behavior in this respect is a strange one, Tindras. I must insist that you ask him before using anything of his."

"We know each other forever, Artias. He doesn't mind—I can assure you he doesn't."

"That may be so, my fellow, but I must insist nevertheless."

The hunter's behavior doesn't even slightly insult or bother Tindras; he looks upon those who approach him and others with respect as good-hearted and fair, and so he agrees with the hunter and sets about finding his kindred spirit. A mere moment passes 'til Gilgaron joins Artias, asking him, "Did you see Tindras? I know he's somewhere around."

"He is looking for you?"

"Is he?"

"Yes. See, I need to use your fireplace but wish to ask you before doing so."

"Go ahead, mine's yours. You help us deal with a terrifying beast, so you shall not feel as if you must ask me for anything—simply take what you need."

"But—"

"Please, hunter, feel free."

"I just appealed to your friend's conscious and now—"

"You did what?"

"Well, I thou—"

"He simply wanted to use my stuff, didn't he?"

Artias says nothing; answering the question would make him feel like if he turn traitor to Tindras, and he is angry at Gilgaron for asking him such a question.

"Ask him," he says angrily, "I am not to tell you! He is your friend, your companion, so dare you ask me a question that could accuse him of doing something unrighteous."

"I was just asking?"

"Most certainly you were."

"Listen, hunter, it never bothered me when he took what he needed, so do not think that I want to accuse him of anything. But, anyway, I wish to ask you something, if I may?"

"You may."

"Say, hunter, did you fight in battle?"

"Why are you asking me this?"

"Because, at times, your words are more such of a warrior than a hunter."

For an instant the thought that his fellow is trying to assess him rushes through Artias' mind. He nevertheless says: "Few of my kin are still alive. Many had died by fighting bandit tribes. Yes, given that, yes, I might be a warrior as much as I am a hunter."

"Bandits, huh? These wicked tribes of theirs rummage the plain and dwell in mountain caves. There is a village in *the northern plain** that was assailed two years ago. Many were slain that day. Your kin, brave men they are fighting these tribes."

"Men and women, my fellow, men and women."

"I shall light the fire, my friend," Gilgaron says as he enters his house. As a sign of friendship he leaves the front door open: Artias shall know that he can step in and out as he pleases.

Arming the sticks with pointed tips, the hunter makes one after the other ready for the evening. When the fire is crackling and burning, Gilgaron emerges from his house again, eager to help Artias taper off the wood. To his amazement, the hunter has already finished and even smiles as he rises, saying, "My knife is sharp."

"Obviously." Taking up a few of the sticks before Artias carries them all inside, Gilgaron returns to the fireplace and sets them down nearby. Ardegan and Tindras come to them then, knocking politely on the open door to signal their arrival.

"Already finished," says Tindras, surprised. He takes one of the sticks, glad to see that the hunter chose beech, continuing, "You made some fine weapons here." He hits the ceiling as he tries to hold the spear erect next to him. "They are long."

"Sadly only seven feet (2.1 meter)," says Artias. "I would've preferred eight."

"Still long enough, really. Arianna's house isn't that big, so I think—well, seven feet may still be too long."

"They have to be this long, because I do not know how long the beast's arms are."

"What beast has seven feet long arms?" Ardegan asks, slightly in worry.

"It is not necessarily the lengths of the arms but the claws extending them," Artias explains and taps on his forearm as he continues: "Some creatures have claws as long as my forearm. Footprints and scratch marks can give you a good first sight at what you are going to deal with."

Everyone around him suddenly hushes. To get sliced open by claws as long as the hunter's forearm would turn their skin inside out and let their guts fall out. They could lose their legs or arms, or be beheaded by one strike. They realize, understand under the horrible imaginations governing their thoughts, what kind of beasts Arjovan actually harbors.

"Makes you feel so vulnerable," Tindras says almost silently.

"You should not think about such things," advises Artias, taking one of the sticks. "Watch." He holds the pointed tip into the flames and turns the stick in his hand. He keeps doing this until the surface of the tapered tip is black in color. "Now it is by far harder than before."

"Where did you learn this?" Ardegan asks. "I am a hunter but did not know—"

"He is a mighty warrior," Gilgaron states, deeming the hunter a good-hearted and skilled man capable of wielding a sword as good as a bow.

"I believe so," says Tindras. When then a thought crosses his mind, his sober voice rises, and he asks anxiously, "The door, what about the front door?"

Aware of what Tindras means, Artias thanks him for his concerns before saying: "I will simply lean the door against its frame."

"Are you mad? Do you wish to be eaten, to get your blood sucked."

"Trust me on this, my fellow."

"We do," Ardegan says and looks at his friends. "Right?"

They agree, saying that they trust the hunter with their lives, and they ask for his guidance, because they do not know what the next step shall be.

"We have the spears," Tindras says, "the trumpet, and a place to bring the people. What's next?"

"It is still day, so do not fear when I ask of you to make a fire in Arianna's house, and please take some firewood with you—we will be needing it."

"I am sure she has firewood."

"I did not see any. Besides, despite that it is day, I do not want to see you walking to her house more than once, and neither do I want you to search for firewood in that area. Go there, take wood along from here, make the fire and return at once—understood?"

"Yes."

"Go together, do not separate and stay wary."

"I say, Artias," Ardegan draws his fellow's attention, "when we made fire, Gilgaron and Tindras part to gather the people, whereas I shall wait for you in her house."

"No, we will go there together, backing each other."

"All right, and what about you? What do you do meanwhile—"

"I will join you after I made the other six ready."

"What?"

"The other sticks, I'll make them ready, or do you wish to make them? You saw how I done it, so you surely can do it, too. I will go with Gilgaron and Tindras to Arianna's house and—"

"No, you make them spears. We are hunters, Artias, like you—have some trust in us."

"It is not trust that I lack but the courage to let you go on your own."

"We can do this." Ardegan looks at his fellows again, asking, "Right?"

"Yes," they say, "we can."

Prowl

He knew: Never would the beast let its eye(s) off its prey and never would it let its quarry get away; to feast it came and feast it shall. Keen eyes were set upon him, letting him feel its presence, and soon he was to witness its savageness.

Before nightfall the people of Odas make their way to the tavern, never letting go their beloveds. Whether they walk alone or in groups, every soul cares for the other, and though they shudder, they try to be alike the brave in their midst.

Gilgaron is awaiting their coming in the tavern, and whomever emerges alone or in company he sends upstairs, and whomever is known for being a noisy fellow he advises to be still, and all those who strike him as clumsy or easily frightened he wants the brave to ward, and as soon as the last few souls have arrived alongside of Tindras, he bars the front door and joins everyone upstairs, bearing three of the spears Artias made upon his shoulder.

"Everything is secured," he tells Tindras and looks at the people continuing: "My friends, do not fear. I say, we will not allow any harm to come to you."

He keeps his eyes set on the crowd for some time and then hands Tindras the spears.

"Come," says he, trudging to the balcony with his bow in one hand and many arrows in his quiver.

"Do you have your knife?" Tindras asks, closing the balcony door with his leg and placing the sticks beside.

"I have it with me—do you have yours?"

"Yes—do you have the trumpet?"

"Yes, got it right here."

"All right. Good. Okay."

They crouch down and roam their eyes over Odas. They will keep doing so until dawn, unless the beast emerges as Artias predicts. In hopes that the hunter and Ardegan are safe in Arianna's house, which is most doubtfully, they remain on guard under arms.

Odas comes into being so quiet, so dark and still while the gloom of night veils their sight and ever noise grows their fright, and they look up at the little they can see of the moon, glad to know that it is whole and casting at least some light upon the ground.

"We should have set torches all across the village," Tindras utters, worried that they might miss to see something creeping around in the dark. "I barely see my own house, and you know it's close by."

"We must use our ears to see."

The night comes with a wave of sounds, sounds they never heeded before tonight, and they tremble slightly with fear to hear the sheer variety of inhuman voices embracing them. Unearthly cries make them shriek, and they wonder how to tell which comes from the creature they await. Both of them are good hunters and have shown courage many times in their lives, but tonight they feel like frightened children. If Ardegan would be with them, they might feel a little less afraid, but he is in Arianna's house with Artias, listening to the sound of the night as his fellows.

TENSE AND UPTIGHT: Ardegan is standing at a window, trying to glimpse through the shutter's angled slats. The giant trees beyond the sheltering wall remain without motion, only their leaves sway by the wind blowing about their trunks and rustle when rain begins to fall upon the greenery.

Artias sees how uptight Ardegan is and how tightly he holds his bow, and he tells him to move away from the window and take a breath.

"I have done this many times before," says he, "so do not fear but rest until—"

"Rest? I dare not look away; it could be out there somewhere just now."

"It most defiantly is."

"You think it is hiding, waiting for the right moment?"

"Yes."

Nodding quickly to himself, Ardegan asks how likely it is that they can fight it off.

Artias shrugs shortly and joins his companion at the window. "If I would know what beast is to come, I could tell you." He looks outside, watching the quivering motion of the leaves. "Dark but not still. I know it is somewhere out there, but it might not necessarily attack tonight."

"You said it will return?"

"I have to take all possibilities into consideration, my fellow."

"How often have you done this?"

"Sitting and waiting, you mean?"

"No, I mean hunting a beast of prey."

"Many a time." This is in fact true. What Artias does not say, though, is that he did not ever hunt a man-eater and neither thought about doing so before he came to Odas. "Should it breach the front—" He hushes and steps closer to the window.

"What?" Ardegan asks, receiving merely a polite but clear gesture to be still.

Outside, within the bushes, Artias heard something moving slowly and steadily. The leaves, the plants, the flora, the noise they cause when something walks by, whether prowling or running, is every so clear. The rain withholds him from hearing much, though what he perceives is enough to make him draw his knife and grab one of the pointed sticks, causing his fellow to gulp and fear an attack.

"What do you hear?" Ardegan asks, trying his utmost to hear what Artias does. "I hear only—"

Yet another gesture signing him to hush is the only answer he gets, and shortly after Artias nods at the remaining sticks, silently telling his companion to grab one, too.

"Keep your eyes on the door," he whispers.

Focused in mind and eye on the brushwood, Artias keeps totally quiet from then on. Holding his knife as if ready for a fight, he glances only once at the front door.

Moments of waiting and shuddering go by until the hunter nods and withdraws from the window.

"It was there," says he. "It knows we are here. It knows we are waiting for it—I am sure."

"Cannot be. No. How could it kno—"

"My friend, you make the same mistake others have made before. Some beasts are capable of thinking to a much greater extent than we assume—I saw creatures evading areas that had been spiked with traps."

"You assume it will come eve—"

"It will come, Ardegan. It will come at the right time."

"What?"

"The night is yet young. We should wait and stay alert."

Knowing that the beast is out there somewhere (probably watching them just now), Ardegan steps away from the window and heads for the fireplace.

A simple metal platter half dug into the ground and surrounded by large and small rocks is used as a fireplace and heater, serving, too, as an oven as well as for drying clothes. Artias sees the advantage the fire gives them in case of an attack and says, "Listen carefully, Ardegan, my fellow, if the beast comes rushing into the house, try to keep the fire between you and it, all right?"

"Oh, I definitely will, but we shouldn't have made this fire as early as we did—it's gonna diminish soon."

"Feed the flames, my fellow, feed the flames."

"We burned all the wood."

Artias hears Ardegan rummaging through the house behind him. Unaware that Arianna keeps all the wood she collects in a small shed outside, he calls his fellow back to him and asks whether he found some firewood, but Ardegan outstretching his arms and shakes his head, telling the hunter that they should have taken more wood along, "'cause, honestly, I have no idea where she keeps hers."

"Perhaps outside?"

"I hope not."

"Maybe she used all of it," says Artias. "I mean, it is not winter."

"But the nights are fresh and windy at times. I tell you, hunter, she is keen on having enough wood—heard her saying so many times."

"Well, then it is outside."

It needs by far more courage to go out than Ardegan can muster. Nevertheless, he asks whether he shall fetch some wood.

"If we are going to get wood, we would need to know where she stores it. Do you know where she keeps it?"

"No," Ardegan says.

"So don't bother getting some."

"But you were the one asking me if it could be outside."

"Just to be informed of possible disadvantages."

"Such as?"

"Having no firewood. You know, actually, we might as well use the furnitures—they are beautifully made, but we should grow the fire."

"No, her father made these—she'll jump at your throat if you hew and burn them."

"So one of us has to go out there and get some wood; or, which would be preferable, we simple stay here and do what we have come here for."

"I simply think that a fire would be helpful. Why don't we take one of the sticks? I mean, we have four, so why not burn one."

"We need these sticks, my friend. They are all that we have to keep the beast away from us."

"True, although it would be nice to have a fire that will not have burned down long before sunrises."

"We do not always get what we want."

"I say, we need a large fire."

"Quiet down, Ardegan—the woods have ears."

With this said, Artias ends the dialogue and focuses back on the area outside in silence. Till deep into the night he remains where he stands, uttering not a single word. His silence worries Ardegan tremendously, and soon his fellow cannot be quiet any longer and asks, "Do you see something?"

"No, but I know it's out there watching us."

Indeed, the beast is watching them. Nicely hidden in darkness, it observes and waits, taking not a pace, making not a sound. With keen eyesight it stares at the closed shutters, knowing by smell that prey is within (easy) reach.

Lurk

Quick it came to seize the unwary, and thought it vanished as fast as it had come, he could see its eyes before he ... no more be the man he had been.

Arianna's house is stable and built of oak, but the door is no more tightly secured to the wall since the attack: it is merely set upright against the wall, using the doorframe to keep it erect.

Sometimes Ardegan simply stands still and spends a few moments looking at the front door, hoping that it will not suddenly fall and unveil what lingers beyond.

"We should have repaired the door," he says.

"Yes, we should have."

"No. Think, my fellow, think. If we would have repaired it, then the beast might try to get in from somewhere else. The door offers no resistance anymore and is therefore the easiest way in."

"It did not seek another way in the first time; and, back then, the door was undamaged."

"I should ask you to trust me, my friend. The creature tried to get in through the wall the night Arianna lost her son. Yes, Ardegan, sometime that night it was trying to get in through the wall when it heard its prey moving about. From what Arianna had told me, I have no reason to assume otherwise."

"And what did she tell you, Artias?" wonders Ardegan, looking grimly at the hunter.

"She said her son approached the front door, my fellow. I imagine the creature heard his tread and went for him straight—I say, let it have its way in."

Ardegan glances at the door resting on its frame: it could be pushed open by a boy without greater effort. He nevertheless understands what Artias means but would prefer to set a trap incase the beast comes to fall upon them when they least expect it.

"We should set up a tarp, just in case."

"No," Artias says, firm in his decision to slay the beast with his knife only. He is too self-confident of his skills as that he would think about a trap. Skilled he is but sadly as foolish. This, at least, is how Ardegan begins to think of the hunter, and he makes known his arousing mistrust.

"Listen," Artias barks angrily, "did you ever see a wounded bear? No? I did, and I tell you, it is far more dangerous than otherwise—trust me, my friend, trust me."

A noise outside lets them both halt their breath and freeze where they stand.

Gesturing Ardegan to be silent, Artias treads carefully to the window, approaching it from the side as silently as he can, and takes a look outside. The dead of night beyond masks the environment, clouding everything within in darkness—he cannot see a thing.

Quickly signing his fellow to ready himself for a possible attack, Artias raises the stick and moves back a pace, his eyes resting on the entrance.

With shaking hands Ardegan lifts the self-made spear and aims the pointed tip at the door, placing the end against the bottom of the wall as he kneels down opposite of the door.

"I am ready," says he.

When Artias trudges to the door to lure the beast in by the sound of his steps, an odd yap—dull, barely louder than a dog's bark—is heard outside. Both men stay still whilst waiting for the beast to come into being. The rain is falling heavily from the skies as another yap reaches their hearing, and shortly after, a penetrating tone drowns out the barks.

"The trumpet!" Ardegan utters loudly, "the trumpet!"

He heads for the front door, driven by the horrid images of his friends' slaying as he tears it open and goes outside. Though Artias cries, "NO, WAIT," Ardegan does not care to listen.

At once the hunter chases after his fellow, running outside as blindly. "WAIT," he keeps yelling in vain up until Ardegan is gone.

Swallowed by the gloom of night, Artias stands in utter darkness, without even a shimmer of light guiding him the way.

"Where are you, my friend," he whispers, "where are you?"

As quietly as he can he looks around, suddenly facing two green eyes in the dark.

The unwary
A vow that was broken, a pledge that seemed a lie let rise the desire to die and made him walk in the shadows of the man he once was and the one he ought to be — righteousness, it dwelled no longer in his heart.

"It knew of our plan. Yes, I am sure of it. It came to Odas, making you sound the trumpet by pretending to enter the tavern."

"No," Tindras cries, quickly looking over to Gilgaron, who tries to calm his fellow citizens. "You will not blame Ardegan's death on us, Artias — he was my friend, a friend I had to bury. A man we had known for many years is now resting in the earth, while you — you who were with him, eager to fight the beast — are among us living souls. Dare you blame me, Artias. Dare you blame us!"

"I do not blame anything on you two. You did the right thing. What I say is that we are dealing with a witted creature."

"It did not take you."

Artias does not know what to say. The beast, it looked him straight into the eyes. All it did was staring at him, glaring at him, resting its eyes on his as if saying, "I see you". It vanished as quickly as it had emerged, and Ardegan was gone. Day's first light unveiled his dead body lying near Arianna's house, not far from where Artias had seen the beast's eyes. It did not feed off his fellow's blood, and it did not take the body along to feed later on. It simply let it lay.

"Say something," Gilgaron shouts, walking away from the people to Artias. "Why did it not attack you? Why did *you* not attack it?"

"You should have killed it," a man yells.

Stepping out of the crowd and shouting "you should have" at the top of his voice, the man draws nearer to Artias, thrusting him. "Why did you not? WHY?"

"OFF WITH YOU." Artias seizes the man by the wrist and brings him to his knees by striking him into the belly. "I SHALL NOT TOLERATE SUCH BEHAVIOR—YOU ARE A GROWN MAN. ACT AS SUCH OR DO NOT SPEAK TO ME!" He then turns to Gilgaron and Tindras before they can assist their fellow and tells them, "Do not force me to fight! I do not blame you for what happened; and yes, yes, I did not strike at the beast, I did not. I WAS FROZEN, STIFF, UNABLE TO MOVE."

The man on the ground rises and starts to speak shamefully about the hunter. He points at him, claiming him a coward, a coward who dared not to move, who dared not to fight, who dared not to drive off the beast and save a life. "HE LEFT ARDEGAN TO THE BEAST FOR FEAR OF DYING HIMSELF."

"I warn you, old man, I warn you, watch what you say!" Artias approaches his tormentor, demanding that he hold his tongue. "I WILL MAKE YOU HUSH IF NEED BE!"

"You call yourself a hunter," says the man, "but you ran away like a child!"

Gilgaron can see Artias' struggles to keep himself from striking the man.

The hunter, who would never leave the life of anyone in the hands of fate, is about to lose his temper and stab down the very man whose words grow the people's mistrust in him. If it weren't for Gilgaron, who tells him to forget the old man and come with him, he probably would.

"Let's go to my house," Gilgaron says, gesturing Tindras to join them.

Artias is grateful for the invitation. The scornful looks all around him make it hard for him to stay calm. He cannot bear the people's judgment nor see that spiteful, old man for a moment longer.

As soon as he enters Gilgaron's house, which made him feel so welcome before, Tindras asks him what he was thinking. He says he shouldn't have struck the man; "it's like telling everyone that he was right."

"As if that matters to you. You believe he is right anyway."

"No, I do not. Gilgaron and I—*we*—merely wonder why it did not take you."

"As if I would know why."

"How could I," Gilgaron mutters, ashamed of himself for treating the hunter as he did, with mistrust: Artias had assisted them and all he did was asking him silly questions, setting him equal to a coward.

"I am sorry," he apologizes. "Can you forgive me my words, Artias. I did not mean to … his passing, it fills me with great sorrow."

"It is forgotten. Tell me, who was that spiteful man who made the people rise against me?"

"Beras is his name. Do not think bad of him. Ardegan was like a son to him. Losing a son is, well—he was not the lord of his words, Artias."

"It is for the best when I leave to hunt the beast on my own. To stay here will only make it harder for everyone."

"I shall join your cause," Gilgaron states.

"What?" Tindras grabs his fellow's arm, urging him to rethink. "You might die."

"I will join him, my friend. Whether you will accompany him or not, I will be going with him."

"You better listen to him," says Artias to Gilgaron. "It could be that we die. You should stay here with everyone else."

"You need my bow and spear."

"All I need is a track."

"I am still coming with you."

"It is your decision, Gilgaron."

Tindras cannot just sit around and hope that either one of them will return, so he decides to go along, too.

"I'm coming too, then," he says shortly. "We track it down and kill it."

"Are you sure about this, my fellows, and I mean you both?"

"Yes, Artias, we are."

"We might be traveling through the forest for some time."

"So?"

"It could be that we die."

"Yes, you said that."

"Okay, listen here, the creatures' realm is full of critters, many of which can kill a grown man; but if you stay wary and keep calm, then we will get through alive."

"The creatures' realm." Tindras wonders what that is, and so does Gilgaron.

"The wilds, my fellows, the wilderness—not Man's realm, simply."

"So you say that we do not belong here?"

"The unwary do not, that's what I say."

"I been in the forest many times," Tindras says. "I never encountered anything larger than a bear."

"Then you were lucky. Besides, man-eaters come at dusk. In winter you might encounter them during the day as well, but lucky for us, plants are in bloom."

"If we see anything, you mean," Gilgaron grumbles, knowing from experience how tightly the forest grows. At certain areas, lush foliage obscures all that lies but a pace ahead.

"The vegetation may be dense," says Artias, "but we will see as little as the creatures."

"Unless they hear better, that is."

"Yes, well, they do; and, um, they have an excellent sense of smell, too."

"Great," Tindras mutters. "Always nice to see how quickly the odds can rise, don't you think?"

"Are you being sarcastic?" asks Gilgaron.

"No, I try to keep my humor from abandoning me."

Together with his two companions Artias makes his way to the small track leading to Arianna's house.

Where Ardegan's body has been found earlier this morning, he stops and closes his eyes for an instant.

"Thank you," he says, unintentionally making his fellows think that he is speaking to them.

"Thank us when we have been victorious," says Gilgaron.

Heedless of the confusion he arouses, Artias continues, saying: "Wherever your soul might be, I hope you rest in peace."

"What?" Tindras comes up to the hunter, asking him what on earth he is talking about. "You wanna make us feel like if we are going to die."

"No, no, I was speaking to Ardegan."

"I see, a last goodbye."

"Yes."

For a moment they remain in silence, and then they begin to search for tracks together.

Whilst thus engaged, Tindras separates from his fellows more and more, inspecting the ground near dense foliage.

"I say, Tindras," Artias calls him on realizing the distance between them. "You should not walk away from us without saying that you do!"

"Come here!"

"Did you hear what I said?"

"Yes, yes, I did. Now come here to me. You have to see this. I found a footprint. Looks alike that of a badger — and insanely big badger."

Artias forthwith hustles to his companion. "A badger you say?"

He crouches down to take a look at the footprint, at a glance realizing that it is alike the one he discovered near Arianna's house. There are two distinctive features besides of the size that unmistakably tell that this footprint was not made by a badger: each claw is significantly large than the other, and there is an extra toe that seems to touch the ground only slightly. Given that he did not see this feature on the first footprint he had found, Artias assumes that the beast was not on the prowl but lying in wait after it lured him and Ardegan outside.

When he seeks to explain his fellows what the footmark tells, the people of Odas emerge walking towards them, shouting about Artias' recklessness.

"Ardegan died, because of you," declares Beras, pointing at the hunter while bringing the people up against him.

"That is not true," Artias states. "He doomed himself by the moment he ran ou—"

"All lies," the people cry. "The beast, you summoned it to take from us our gold for its killing!"

"I never asked for your gold. I never wanted anything else than to warn you of beasts of prey. I wish only to make known the importance of a stockade—in Odas more than anywhere. You people, you live within the creatures' realm, where not a soul can tell what prowls about."

His words find no hearing. With united voices the people cry at him that the truth of his coming shall be revealed through a simple test. The say, "We shall tie you to a tree, and then, then we will see whether you summoned it or not—your death shall prove you haven't."

As much as Gilgaron and Tindras mourn for their fellow's death, they cannot abide Beras' behavior. Since they know him, his demeanor was calm. Now, though, his pain, the sorrow for the passing of a man he had looked upon as a son, governs his way of thinking, making him turn wicked and in need of a face to blame.

"Do not let your pain speak for you," they tell him, but Beras already has herded the people around him, making them his allies in his very own foul call for justice.

"The beast," Beras says, "the beast did not take him. Why did it not kill him like it killed Ardegan?" He turns to the people then and continues in a way so wicked that Gilgaron and Tindras struggle to recognize him as the man he was. "It slew our friend and let his body lay. But whose body was not next to Ardegan's? It was the hunter's. Artias lives and breathes and laughs at us because of our blindness to see who brought this peril upon us! I tell you, he wants our gold and then, when we have given it to him, you will see how quickly he will vanish with a smile on his face and bags full of gold, our gold. It is on us to end this, and it shall end, it shall end with his death—I say, tie him to a tree."

"NO," cries Tindras, "Ardegan was my friend, but his death is not Artias' fault. The creature is witted. It tricked—"

"Oh, I see, Tindras, I see how he manipulated you into believe that his cause is righteous. You and Gilgaron, how can you be so bl—"

"ENOUGH," shouts Artias. "I DID NOT MANIPULATE ANYONE, AND I WILL NOT ALLOW YOU TO BLAME ME FOR—"

"THIS IS OUR HOME, OURS, AND YOU WERE A GUEST. WE BELIEVED YOU, TRUSTED YOU. NOT ANYMORE, ARTIAS. YOU HEAR, WE TRUST YOU NO MORE, BECAUSE WE SEE AND UNDERSTAND, AND WE WILL TAKE ACTIONS."

Tarion, the old man Artias approached as he had arrived at Odas, is among Beras' allies and says that something always seemed strange about the hunter. "You are not how you give yourself," he says. "You arms are too strong for a hunter and your height is too great, and you—"

"And my hair? Are my hair too short or my eyes too small? IS MY PACE NOT QUICK ENOUGH OR MY BOW NOT USED ENOUGH!"

"HE IS MOCKING US," yells Beras. "HE CALLS, THINKS US FOOLS, PRIMITIVE, HALFWITTED FOOLS."

All Artias wanted was to help these people. He stood steadfast, was brave and courageous for every soul he had been trying to ward; and yet, after all his endeavors, he has been blamed for everything that had befallen already, and now he is even deemed a deceiver—he can only just bear such cruelty.

And he tells Beras that he did call after Ardegan, that he shouted at him to wait. "At the top of my voice I cried at him," he says.

"OH, YOU, YOU WICKED SOUL LURED THE BEAST TO HIM!"

"HOW DARE YOU SAY—" In rage Artias draws his knife, thrusting it into his tormentor's throat. In rage he dives it through the flesh, shoving and forcing it through muscles and bone. "YOU HATEFUL, OLD MAN! YOU ARE THE WICKED SOUL HERE!"

Nobody tears him away from Beras, not even Gilgaron or Tindras do anything. They cannot believe what they see, and neither can Artias, who steps away from the man he just slew, with brooding eyes looking at his hands. He pledged to himself to protect the people Beras was among.

"No ... no ," he stammers, "no ... I did not want ... no. I wanted to help only!" The knife glides out of his hand as he moves away from the body, abhorred of his outburst. "I did not want this—no, no." Slowly he withdraws into the forest, and then he runs, runs without end until his breath is gone and his legs refuse to even walk.

Resolution

There he awoke to the truth and wanted to make known the cause for the path he had chosen to walk forth on, and yet would those who he called his fellows deem him mad.

No other than huge they have grown to this day, casting shade upon the lush green beneath them and all the flowers blooming in their cover. Anchored to the earth with roots taller than men, with sturdy boughs and large trunks, these trees have come to dwarf beech and oak; and as an army they stand, forming an ancient woodland, a vast and brilliant forest down south.

When the first men came to this land, beholding the greatness of nature and the bounds of the forests beyond which lie great plains, seeing the mountains that come forth as a resemblance of eternity, and feeling the great winds that carried every seed of every plant away, all and everything that came into being was thought to be everlasting.

And there trudging across these lands is a man, Artias, who perceives little of the glories of this realm; he cannot stop brooding over Beras' accusations, these words of incrimination that penetrated his heart, arousing an urge to act, a pressing desire to have him brought to silence. Henceforth engulfed in darkness, blood drenched the knife's blade at his awakening, dripping from its edge and tip; and his hands have been shaking ever since.

In vain trying to see why, oh, why was he treated with such revulsion by the people, his thoughts soon come to rest upon their blindness. Why were they blind to his care but open to a lie ... why did they blame him, come together to curse him, set to hurt him … . Why did they want his death, seeking only his death while being blind to the endeavors he took upon himself to ward them … above all, "I came to your aid."

But the words of one man have poisoned them all and let spite spread root in them. The pain is soon all over dominating his very thought, and his heart bleeds and his mind bids farewell; and he trudges on through the forest, crying out his misery.

In his suffering he forgets to be conscious of the realm of beast. When treading this kingdom unwarily, death can be swift; and death is indeed approaching him, creeping towards him, advancing at his ever step.

Preyed on by what he sought to slay, an instant of awareness awakens him to the critter on his tail. Straight facing the shape he espied lurking in the undergrowth, he witnesses the beast creeping out of the green, shocking him into silence by its sheer appearance.

Frozen, stiff once more, he can only gape at this bizarre being before him, which face comes forth with no mouth nor nose 'til the flesh covering its jaws rises and unveils a hideous maw. To see this fearful gaping jaw with ever so many small and large teeth strikes fear into Artias' heart.

Clenching his fists, mustering his courage, he shouts at the beast to begone in terror.

"I WILL COME FOR YOU SOON ENOUGH!" cries he and steps back, taking an arrow out of his quiver to use it for a knife. "I WILL NOT BE SLAIN BY YOU, MONSTER—NEVER!"

The beast does not attack nor withdraw: it simply stands still while looking at him and the pointed end of his arrow. Its eyes reveal no hate, not a glint of wickedness, not a shine of lust for his death—much unlike Beras, whose eyes made seen his thirst, his baneful yearning for Artias' end.

"What are you waiting for?" Artias asks the great critter, confused about its behavior. "Come now if you dare!"

But the beast, though seemingly inclined to devour him, trudges off, withdrawing into the plant life—which should awaken Artias to the ugly truth. While observing its retreat, the purity of its existence dawns on him, enlightening him to the truth.

For a while he stands rooted to the spot in astonishment, hoping to be shown, in whichever way, what he ought to do now that he has been given enlightenment. And he wonders whether he should proceed or cease his undertaking.

Not far from him someone's footfall attracts his attention, focusing his mind back on to his surroundings, and thereupon he hears Tindras calling him. Almost immediately he follows his fellow's voice, holding the arrow in firm grasp.

Catching sight of his friend through the leafage, he hustles through a wall of bushes straight to him.

"Artias," says Gilgaron, all at once emerging behind the hunter with a bow in hand. "Good we found you."

"If you seek to avenge—"

"No," Tindras hisses. "We told you we will help you take down the beast, and that we shall."

"But did you not see, did you not see what I have—"

"Right now I worry more about the beast than I see sense in thinking about what you did."

"But the people, they will—"

"Look, Artias, we are here, equipped with bows and knives, willing to help you hunt. Neither one of us wishes to talk about what you did. We deal with the beast and then part ways."

Tindras reaches behind his back and brings the hunter's knife to light and thereupon hands him the weapon, saying, "You will be needing it."

Knowing that what he did cannot be forgotten nor forgiven, Artias demands that his fellows leave him alone and return to Odas straight. His fellows, though, do not comply but say, "We are here because we told you we will help you. Do not dare to send us away now," and they order him to take the knife. "You will be needing it."

Even though Artias rather not take his knife, he does so; and in sorrow he then speaks to them, saying, "With this knife I killed your friend. Listen, my fellows—"

"No, Artias, there is nothing to say! Just let us search for the beast and—"

"I encountered it not far from here. It walked off not long after I shouted at it."

"What? You say you saw—"

"I say I let it walk away, and I say that it must have known that attacking me could mean an injury, which to have would be fatal."

Tindras lays an arrow on his bow, preparing for the case of a sudden attack by the creature.

"Fatal?" he utters confusedly. "What do you mean by 'fatal'?"

"I mean it must have known that a simple injury can be its death. Injured it cannot hunt effectively. Given that I managed to scare it off quite easily, I presume that it relies on killing its prey quickly to avoid a fight."

"So all we need is one strike."

"I do not know if it can be killed so easily. I saw its jaws. It has teeth, but what has teeth does not feed off blood only. No. It eats meat, but—"

"You said it feeds off blood."

"It could be that it does not waste any nutrition. I think it sucks the blood of its prey before devouring the flesh."

"We shall hunt it down," Gilgaron cries. "We shall kill it for what it did."

But Artias states that nobody shall seek to harm the beast, for all it did was hunting to survive, and he says that if ever there was a being that is to be brought to the sword for injustice, then it had not come from the creatures' realm.

"Its eyes," he tells his fellows, "in its eyes there showed not a glint of wickedness!"

"Evil to the core," Tindras utters furiously. "It shall and will pay for—"

"You want its death for the wrong reasons. It may be that we—you and everyone in Odas—are to blame for the boy's passing only! Yes. A stockade, my fellows, a stockade could have prevented all that had happened."

"How dare you, Artias!" Gilgaron shouts, fuming at such an insult. "We are not to blame for—"

"You are to blame! You and every one of Odas, because none of you care to see!"

To himself Artias then mutters, "Why did I not see the wickedness in you, in you both," and at them he shouts, "You are the monsters! You and your kind!"

A hush descends over his fellows, and they gape at each other, with worries muttering, "What happened in Arianna's house."

"I say, I have been awakened to a truth—an ugly truth, and I have realized whose to be deemed a beast."

"You have no right to call either one of us a—"

"We bring about suffer and chaos. We are those whose deeds, whose greed and needs, destroy the natural balance. We are beast—me, you, we all are!" Now only anger is his drive, and the righteousness he had been striving to uphold lies no longer in his heart; and he cries, "ONLY MANKIND TAKES JOY IN KILLING."

"What's wrong with you?" Gilgaron wonders, saying something the hunter would not heed as enraged as he is: "Perhaps we shall … what could have been done … ."

"I tell you here and now: Hound the beast and I shall cut you down." At once Artias holds his knife aloft. "WITH THIS BLADE I WILL!"

His fellows are utterly confused about Artias' sudden outburst. He wanted to kill the creature as much as they, but now he protects it, fights for it as if to kill it would be an act of murder. What they do not know is that the creatures' realm is like a village to Artias, it is the home of beast, which to enter and wherein to live means to take and accept the risks as they are. Too late he realized that his own strive to kill it was wrong, simply, and he asks his fellows: "Do you think that you and me, as the hunters we are, have the right to chase down a beast and kill it although it merely does what we have been doing all our lives, hunting? What if we hunt a deer and are then being hunted ourselves for doing so?"

"Why are you defending it, Artias?" Gilgaron strikes the brushwood with his foot, crying, "IT KILLED HER SON, AND YOU, YOU SAID IT WILL RETURN—"

"I was a fool, but now I see. To hunt it down is wrong, because it has done us no wrong!"

"IT KILLED HER SON!"

"And we kill deer and rabbits and badgers or hunt for big game, and although we do so, we have never been preyed upon because of that! Only we, *we* seek revenge, strive to avenge, try to establish dominion! It is wrong! Do you not see, my fellows? Why do you not see!"

It is fear that made Tindras and Gilgaron seek the beast's death: the fear of being attacked, of losing someone close; the fear of death dominates their thoughts, and they will not allow Artias to prevent them from saving those who could be taken by the beast in the days to come, and so it comes that Tindras raises his bow, aiming at Artias as he says, "It might be for the best when you go on your way, hunter, and—"

"I cannot."

"Do not make me release this arrow just ye—"

"Forgive me, my friend, but I cannot allow you to harm the creature!"

"Damn you, Artias," Gilgaron yells. "What has gotten into you!"

"It dawned on me, and then I realized and understood that what we do is wrong."

"You have no idea what is going on here, hunter!"

"Dorhyé neh art Wann (*Do not be a beast*)."

"I do not speak *Nahess**, Artias, " Gilgaron says, "and I do not have to hear a word more of your nonsense. I thought you a fine man, a splendid warrior, but I was wrong! Perhaps I should be thankful, for it is easier to deal with a madman."

Artias refuses to listen to them, and he will not draw back nor let them pass: come what may, he will stand steadfast. And he holds his knife at them, saying (that) "If must be, I will use my blade to stop you."

His fellows have about enough.

"As if that would change anything," they say.

Oddly gazing at the hunter, Tindras advances towards him.

"You are such a fool, Artias," says he. "Do you know for wh—" Stumbling over a root jutting partly out of the earth, he hits hard upon the ground, releasing the arrow.

Seeing but the arrow flying by the hunter's neck, Gilgaron utters, "You missed!" And he forthwith lets his bow fall and attacks Artias with drawn knife.

"I stab him down!" cries he, lunging forwards many times to thrust the blade into his foe's gut. All at once thumped in the face, he sways and moves back, feeling his blood running into his mouth.

"Damn you!" he blusters. "Damn yo—"

With the arrow in one hand and the knife in the other, Artias sets upon him, booting his knee, breaking the cap, straight ramming the arrow into his neck.

"Why did you attack me?" he shouts, driving the arrowhead deeper into the flesh. "Why, why, why!"

Tindras, yet lying on the ground, rises as quickly as he can, moving anxiously to the body of his fellow.

"You killed him," he yells. " You killed him!"

"He attacked me! I, I had to—"

"Oh, you will pay for this!"

Bursting with anger, Tindras grasps a rock and comes at Artias, trying shatter his skull with one blow. Well versed in fighting, Artias dodges the strike, straight countering with his knife.

When he leaves the site of the fight, dawdling through the forest, he wipes the blood off his knife with his palm.

"Why did you not listen to me," says he and sheathes his knife, trying to see his deeds as righteous. He nevertheless struggles greatly with what he did and halts after an hour of walking to look at the sky and ask himself whether he should have simply done as they had told him. Maybe it would have been wiser, maybe not. He does not know.

Silently he pulls his knife out of its sheath again, staring at the blade with which he killed two men this day, and he asks himself, "How could I let myself do something like … ." Thinking of his uncle to whom he always said as a little boy that on day he will be a hero, he is abhorred of himself and throws this fine knife away.

Mutual
Whoever they were, truly fine man they had to be to never waver where others would have — as he said, with sorrow in his voice, they were like brothers.

Upon the mountain where ice, snow and rock harden a travel across, there are five men — all strong fellows, with bodies clothed in armors — trudging through the snow while talking about all that will change when they have found whom they seek.

"No more I will feel her hate then; I will be standing with him, doing right not wrong, and I shall have found my way again — yes, I will be virtuous again."

"We all shall find our way out of this darkness we have been living in for so long."

One of them battered a man to death over an argument. A shopkeeper had accused him of stealing merchandise whenever visiting a store and he lost his temper thereupon.

And those he travels with have been vile to others too, beating whomever had deemed them to be wicked with staff or fist, pounding on when they lay on the ground, to death if so they please.

Burglary, murder, vandalism, death threats (many of which they performed), passing water before a tavern, scaring traders into handing them goods for free, these five men are regarded as through and through evil. But their doings had a beginning, a source that caused them to brawl and thereon rob and thereon kill. They had not always been the man they have become. A few years ago they were honest souls working hard from dawn to dusk. Among Arjovan's neighboring countries there is but one that is just, the others are horrid places for those who are born into poverty, like these five men were. But the times they had been breaking their backs to earn but one gold coin that would be taken from them the same day for taxes were over when heralds had arrived, telling them and others of a land where all life below the Sun is equal. And they departed for Arjovan the following day with others; yet, throughout their journey, they encountered people who had considered leaving your motherland to live elsewhere a treacherous act. Although to leave the land would have only been a violation of the law if they had owned a store, fields, or grounds; more than a few of those they had been with, among them the heralds, were hanged. The way to the border was one horrible undertaking. They were called "castoffs", and rocks were thrown at them, and they, though trying to stay honorable, could soon bear no more hatred other than their own. The words of others had broken them and reformed them, and they made people fear them from that day forth; and they continued their path even upon arriving in Arjovan, until the deeds of one man made them wish to be what no more they were.

"I say, we must find him."

"They say he is somewhere beyond this mountain, or maybe even somewhere east—"

"Enough of this!" says the man in the fore of the group. "We have been told where he was going."

"Yes, Gordes, we have been told. 'Somewhere south,' they said, 'beyond the mountain'—how is that supposed to help us."

"We are drawing nearer with each step. Wait until we see the region before you complain!"

Oddity

All alone he was when there showed a figure in the distance, and when the being arouse, he felt as if his eyes were misleading him.

Artias is quick—however silent his tread—and has been traveling for two days until now, at dawn of the third reaching a glade where a river streams through the green. And there the mountains rise before him, towering into the sky. As a monument they stand, a remembrance of bygone days, a testament to the age of the ground he walks upon. These mountains always made him continue his path in spite of the odds. But a glance of their greatness would always inspire him to move on, though this be no more now, for he has come off his way.

He is adrift and alone, looking upon himself as a rogue who has no right to speak of virtue. He is but a slayer, a man whose rage ceased his demeanor, a man of foulness whose wrath threw him off his way down into the abyss of shame. No more shall he wander; no more shall he ward; no village shall he visit forth on, and no soul shall ever again hinge his faith upon this vile man, for he has given in to ire.

"But I wished to be righteous," says he. "Throughout all my days I have tried to do right"—he halts in his tracks, gazing at the mountains—"for I shall be just to every being below the Sun."

He can only just calm his troubled self and heads on across the glade in his misery, longing for guidance in these hours of darkness. If only he had a way to escape this ordeal, then he could lie in the shade and summon his spirits.

Feeling a breeze upon his skin, he observes the swaying grass, looking at himself as one of these blades, but one that is moldering, slowly dying until taken in by the earth: he is a plant bearing no seed, a river carrying no water—he is a case of flesh sheltering a wounded heart.

Certain to have lost his way, for he had led himself astray, he proceeds towards the riverbank, there at its edge espying what seems to be a man who is quenching his thirst. He keeps up his pace, at his ever step seeing just how mighty this stranger appears to be. Though crouched over, this fellow is of astounding stature and reveals to be hardbodied as he arises. He may be a warrior, a soldier of foreign grounds searching for fame or foe; though by and by enlightened to the truth, Artias sees this being as neither man nor beast: its skin is as gray as ash and by a look at its face at a clear day, the semblance to a human is ever so clear and yet do its eyes remind of a critter.

Standing erect at the riverbank, the being raises its head, staring at the mountains in silence as if there be a bond between it and these vastly rising grounds of rock and earth; and more than once its eyes are drawn to the southeast, whence it might have come.

Straight lowering its head, the creature remains standing with bowed head. Aware of Artias' approach, it heeds his tread; and on having discerned his position, it turns to face him, seeing a figure, a small, frail being seeking the river.

"I mean no harm," says Artias. "I only wish to drink."

Whilst glancing at the creature, he crouches down, diving his hands into the water. At ever glance he takes at this critter, he can see how closely it is watching him, and he almost falls into the river on discovering that it is bearing a blade: never before in his life has he seen a creature carrying a weapon.

Until he steps away from the river, it literally stares at him and then walks away along the bank.

Unable to believe what he sees, Artias forthwith follows the beast, amazed at how it emerges and awed by its presence. He believes to see something that comes from a place no human can reach: the heavens. Somewhere beyond the clouds there must be something, something that created all the things around him, something that watches over everyone and that guides ever being walking upon the earth, flying through the skies, swimming the seas, or crawling through the soil, and he believes to see just this very being.

"Wait," he yells after it, "wait," but the beast does not slow down.

Struggling to keep up at its pace, he foolishly starts to run. And straight turning around upon perceiving his approach, the entity darts to him and seizes him by the throat, at once raising him aloft; and he, though depending upon its mercy to live forth, can only look at its blue eyes, these clear blue eyes. He feels neither pain nor fear when it lets him fall.

"Can you forgive me?" asks he, his throat sore from being raised off the ground. "Forgive me, I beg of you."

"Voranias," says the beast, arousing yet more astonishment in the hunter.

Again it turns away from him and walks on its way, but he cannot let it get away and hustles after it, asking over and over for its forgiveness. Unfortunately, he is not aware of what he is dealing with; and when he takes off his bow to lay it down, the beast raises its blade and draws to him, screeching horridly as it comes at him.

"NO!" cries he, falling to his knees and placing the bow on the ground in front of him. "Please, accept my weapon in token of my shame. I desire to change the path I walk. I beg of you, forgive me—can you not see my suffering!"

His words appear to bring the beast to a sudden stop, and it looks at him with gnashing teeth, then saying, "Can you."

"Can I what?" Artias utters excitedly. "Say, what do you wish me to do?"

"What, I, wish ... you, to do."

"Please, tell me."

"Tell, what, wish, can. Dirio... Anhe,jar.telra vodess."

"I do not understand. Do you speak Nahess?"

"Nahess. Bastora. we,tar."

"E ast (for) Ataness (*I ask* (for) *forgiveness*)."

The beast grumbles and then growls, looking as if it wonders what this little man is saying. In a loud voice it then speaks, saying: "Wantas. Want, wish. Dirio. Tell, can. Handro tajrhal josre,daje'r."

"Can hou Atane mey (*Can you forgive me*)."

The beast, bigger than him and by far more powerful, grabs Artias' shoulder and raises him to his feet.

"Stahotes," it says and walks away.

Neither of both has any idea what the other is saying. Whereas the creature is aware of this, Artias is not and keeps asking for forgiveness. He doesn't care whether or not it would kill him. It does not matter to him anymore now. He simply does not care. All he sees is this divine creature that has the power to forgive him. But he cannot keep up as it heads on and soon loses it out of his sight.

Yet, longing to see it again, he returns to the glade and waits for three days in hopes that it may reemerge—which it does not. For however long he could survive at the edge of this glade (for he has fare, water, shade, and a host of trees to ascent for a night's rest), he is no fool who would linger around to his dying day; moreover, he feels as if he has already been given blessing and guidance, for he was brought to his feet by a divine being. On bended knees he had offered it his weapon as a symbol of his shame, desiring to be granted the chance to change his path; but instead of taking the bow, it raised him to his feet. Ever since yesterday he has come to regard this as a command, the command to proceed with his undertaking; and now he is firm in his decision to return to Odas and face whatever may await him there. He does not even care about his bow, which he left behind in the woods, although it is truly a fine one, engraved with his name and made of the finest wood ever to have shaped a hunter's bow.

Fellowship
Where his pain had begun, there he found empty grounds ... and fellowship.

To approach the spot where he had slain his fellows, reawakens the pain he dispelled; and the urge to vomit rouses at the sight of the blood he shed: the blood of his fellows reddened the ground, and though their bodies were claimed by beast', the blood remained, dry and not washed away by rain.

Artias believes that the only way in life is to be righteous and never lie; therefore, he must tell the people (of Odas) what happened to their fellows, Gilgaron and Tindras; and yet when he returns to Odas, he is the only soul there, for all who had once dwelled here have left; but they wrote a letter before leaving which was signed by every man and woman who could write and hung to attract whomever may pass by. The letter is nailed on a post nearby a house, catching his attention as he walks through the village, dreading to think what could have betide; and in this letter he should find a horrid lie:

This village is abandoned, and you, whoever you are, you shall know that this village — Odas, our home — once was a peaceful place; but, blighted by a hunter who brought with him a beast that he made kill a boy, it is now a grave. His name, the hunter's name, is...

Artias cannot read a further word — it is too painful to discover what awful illusions the people have had since Ardegan's death. To think that he unleashed the beast upon them is but a distasteful accusation without equal and to him as if a thousand arrows pierce his heart. To even assume that he would have the power to summon a beast is far off truth and thought—it is disgusting. Nonetheless, he is not sure if he could have been their guardian. He doubts it; seeing that he killed is allies, he may be no other than a liar. Yes. Maybe they are right; maybe he did bring a beast with him, the beast in him. Maybe. Sadness strikes tears into his eyes, and the tears he sheds fall upon the letter and wash the charcoal off the paper. In sorrow he walks on along the path through Odas, thinking about the day of his arrival, as he tread just this very path for the first time.

At the heart of the village, he sits down upon the ground, asking himself what he shall do. What if Tarion or any of the others who have turned against him will decide to pay someone to hunt him down. If that happens, he will always have to be on guard, no matter where he goes: no day there will be without foreboding then.

"I say, hallo," he hears a voice saying and forthwith turns around, dreading to see who there might be.

A group of five men—all fearsome, hefty warriors who know how to survive a fight to death—come towards him, asking him why he is sitting on the ground.

"Who are you?" asks he, looking at their leather armors and steel swords. "What do you want?"

One of the five men is carrying Artias' bow in his hand and lays it down next to the hunter, inquiring, "Is this yours?"

"What? Where did you—"

"Is it yours?"

"Yes, but—"

"So you are Artias, huh? I must say, finding you was quite a quest."

Artias cannot imagine that anyone could have put a bounty on his head in this short time. These men must have been sent by someone else, someone who doesn't know of the events in Odas.

"Who sent you?" he wonders.

"Nobody. We have heard of your deeds. Wandering the land to warn the people of beasts, I believe that a brave undertaking."

"I do not understand."

"Come now, up with you." The man rises and waits 'til the hunter is on his feet before explaining: "We traveled a far way to find you, eager to assist you. If you are who you say you are, that is. So are you Artias?"

"Yes."

"I must say, a fine bow you have there, Artias, engraved with your name, made of yew, with a good grip and a strong string bending the wood, and spikes at the recurved end. A fine bow indeed—you should not lose it again. Anyway, let me introduce myself. I am Gordes and these are my companion—"

"Do not speak a further word. I slew my disputer in rage, killed my allies to ward a beast. I say, know whom you travel with, Gordes—I am not as good as you may think."

"I killed my father two years ago, and my men, do ask them what they have done."

"What have they done?"

One of the others steps forth, introducing himself as Hentario and showing Artias the many notches on his sword. He says that many of these come from the slaying of both the wicked and the good-hearted.

The eyes of an honest fellow look at Artias as Hentario explains that he is no man who would commit malevolent deeds but the words of others had caused him to be open to evil.

"I remember the night of my ordeal ever so clear," says he. "I have been called a 'castoff' for years, though tried to stay virtuous despite the injustice I had to bear. I could take no more after that night. The night of my ordeal, the woman haunting me in my dreams. I heard her screaming for help, crying out to every soul near and far for help and dashed into the house out which had come her cries. With a torch in my hand, willing to do what I must to save her, I drew my blade in sight of a man rummaged through the house. I took him down, not knowing that he was just searching for a candle as his wife feared the dark. I believed to see a villain and acted. To this day, she curses me to die, joining in the shouts of all who call me a castoff—I can feel her hate every day.

But I tried to help. All I did was trying to help. I see nevertheless the pain I had caused with that. I knew how the people think of me, speak of me, and I allowed their words and thoughts into my heart from that night forth, and I began to be what never I dared—now, that is no more. It shall be no more."

Another one of these five fellows says that he once struck down whom he thought a thief. Showing Artias a knife with a truly uniquely curved blade, he says that he cut his throat with this.

"I could not know that he had not stolen my coin pouch but merely wished to return it to me. Yes, I did kill him as he gave me the pouch, heeding not a word he spoke as I cut him down. All who had spoken to me before did so only to insult me, which drove me into believing that he was no better than others. I cared not about him when I forced my knife over his flesh. Sometimes I try to imaging how it would have been if I hadn't acted blindly. Whenever I do, I am reminded of my foulness anew. As my fellows do, so do I—we grief, wish to draw back from the evil in us and find our way again, for we have come off it long ago."

All the man before Artias had tried as best as they could to brawl whenever they possibly could, 'til that alone did not suffice to ease their hate. Because of all the wrong that had been done unto them, hatred grew whenever they were mistreated, and with it rose the need to go even worse to bear the bane of not being loved.

"We vowed to be feared," they say. "Oh, how did we enjoy to see our foes lying in the dirt, begging us for mercy. Triumph, it was our only drive."

"Yes," cries a man in their midst. "I was claimed a thief by a shopkeeper. As much as I tried to make him see that I had not taken anything of his, he would not listen, even called me a liar; but thereon he should utter his last words, for when I began to batter him, he would cry at me to stop—no more I could, to his death, into his grave, I battered forth."

Each of these man's eyes display their pain, unable to be hidden behind their masquerade, and Artias can't but feel compassion, for he had seen men like them before. A hollow stare, a look into the empty, a mere word spoken without reason to other than them; at times turning silent, brooding, thinking of their hardship and that caused by them; and the smile, the bliss to know that those they are among are their dearest, their fellows where others are not—hardship can reach down to the very soul; and when one is broken, fellowship is heaven, a heaven they have found in mutual suffering.

Gordes sprawls his arms, telling Artias, "We did not enjoy being feared. Not one of us wanted to be what we have become. It were the words, the scowls and stones thrown at us that brought us off our way and turn wicked. I believe we are alike you, Artias." Gordes then says that as they have heard of a hunter who ventures from village to village to help the people, they saw their chance to change the path they walk and become righteous and honorable in heart. "You may guide us, hunter, 'cause you are righteous, and you are honorable."

"We wish to follow you and stand with you," says Hentario, "and if need be, we shall die with you."

"Be warned," says Artias; "the face of death seems to follow in my shadow."

"There are things worse than death, Artias," utters Gordes.

"Are you sure you wish to join me?"

"We are!" say all five men.

"So be it, then. The sky is darkening, I say we stay here and move on at day's first light."

"As you say."

The small group heads for the tavern at once and checks whether there is something to drink anywhere immediately on entering.

While the sky darkens rapidly, they make fire in the fireplace and shortly after sit together at a table, discussing where to go tomorrow and drinking as if there be no tomorrow. There are no villages near Odas which means they will have to travel a long way through the creature's realm. However, Gordes wonders about something that did not let him go ever since he had arrived at Odas.

"Where are the people?" he asks. "This village does not seem to have been abandoned very long ago."

"The people left, because they thought I let a beast come upon them."

"A beast?"

"Yes, a great beast that feeds off flesh and blood. It hunts by night as it seems, although I have encountered it during the day as well."

Gordes and the others feel slightly uncomfortable now that they hear of the man-eater prowling about Odas. To their relief, Artias says that it may not return anymore, because "There is no one here anymore."

"No one?" Gordes leans back in his chair, stating that there are six hearty men sitting at a table: "A feast for a beast."

"True, yes, but fear not. I doubt it will return," says Artias, almost certain that it will not come back; nevertheless, after a spell, heavy footsteps are heard beyond the tavern's walls.

Gordes, a man who cannot be frightened easily, unsheathes his sword silently and approaches the window, closely followed by his most trusted companion, Hentario. While he tries to catch a glimpse of the area outside, he signs the others to check the rooms in case there are any openings they do not know about.

"There is no need to slay it," says Artias. "We may only fight if attac—"

It is a yelp that lets Artias hush and the others shriek and move back a pace, and thereupon a powerful screech, which quivers in their ears and sends shivers down their spines, follows the first; and then a roar is heard among growls and grunts and they assume to be about to face not one but two man-eaters and ready themselves for the worst.

Everyone apart from Artias hold their blades in their hands and throw over tables to have a barrier behind which to stand and fight.

"Ready your bow," Gordes tells Artias, who shakes his head and treads to the front door, at once tearing it open.

"WHAT ARE YOU DOING?" cries Hentario.

None of the five men knows that the hunter had recognized the screech and opened the door only to see *the divine being** again; and, indeed, he sees it emerging from the dark into the light he cast outside by opening the door; and he sees the man-eater, that odd and bizarre creature merely a few feet away from it. The blade of the holy being is magnificent through and through, and he sees words and symbols engraved on it, and when he witnesses how these tow mighty creatures come up against each other, he beholds the supreme force of what he deems a god and watches it fight the man-eater and taking it down in less than an instant.

"By all that I have ever seen," Gordes says, staring at the great creature from behind the tables.

"Stay here," Artias utters excitedly and, despite his companion's warnings to stay where he is, walks straight at the creature.

Looking at him, the entity lowers its blade.

"Voranias. Watch you," it says and grabs its catch before walking away into the darkness of the night. With bated breath Artias watches it vanish, unable to look at anything else than this holy being, and even as it is seen no more, his eyes keep looking.

A brave Man
Told of his deeds that made known his name, he was claimed to be brave, even deemed a hero, yet the days to come were to show whether he was.

Until dawn Artias and his companions talk about what they have seen: a creature, a manlike being that bears a weapon has never been witnessed before.

Artias keeps telling the others that it must be divine. He says it is "something that lives in the heavens".

"It killed the beast so quickly," Gordes comments, still thinking about the swiftness of its attack, and he then says to Artias, "I do not know what it is, but we shall never forget this night."

"I wonder, why, why did that bizarre critter not attack me?" says Artias. "In the forest it had withdrawn for fear of a wound that could prevent it from hunting; so why, why would it fight the divine one tonight?"

"Sometimes you have no other choice than to fight," says Gordes and tells Artias of a man who had been chasing after him so relentlessly for so long than he had to kill him to get him off his tail.

"I remember that hunt," says Hentario, "but it might as well be that the creature tried to creep up on that manlike beast and was, therefore, slain straight—who's to say, who's to ask."

"By the way," Artias utters, "it may be that the people of Odas wish to see me dead. I assume they will try to find someone who will—"

"Then they shall do so," Gordes declares, thumping the table with his fist, "and we, we shall drive off whoever comes."

And Hentario smiles as he tells Artias, "Your deeds are well known to the people in this land. The dangers you face on your daily travels and the risks you take for your fellows are held in high regard. If I were you, I wouldn't worry about anyone. The people we met on our travels said you are a hero."

And the others say, "Whatever may be, fear not; you are not alone, Artias, not now nor ever you shall be—we back our fellows."

Happening
Always, to the end of his days, he would say: Who I thought had wished to slay me, for he said he would; on the turn, came to be one of my dearest ... .

A group of people, many of whom seem agitated and move warily for fear of drawing attention, are wandering through the forest, terrified of the realm they are in. They are hungry, in need of rest, and afraid; but regardless of how many tell her, "We should have never left Odas," Arianna keeps guiding them farther away from the village, assuring everyone in her care, "We are close—I am sure."

"How can you know?" say the people. "Death will shadow on us at nightfall—we shall not risk our beloveds' life."

"Just why do you allow fear into you? Since Artias had told you of critters, you have been risking your beloveds more than ever before."

"No," cries a voice—the voice of a young man, a man who knows that he alone cannot fight off a beast, for he knows not how to wield a blade or use a knife or handle a bow. "We are aware of—"

"No, you are not aware of anything. And if you were, you would trust me and not speak in such a loud voice—you mustn't yell, unless you wish to have us set upon."

"But, no," says the lad, "never I would."

"Then you shall be still for the others' safety."

Arianna draws a breath, not knowing for how much longer she can keep everyone from abandoning her. And from underneath her cloak she takes out a dagger, looking at the blade and cursing whose name is engraved upon. Thinking of this man, who slew her mother and many more, she says, "You made me what I am!"

"Arianna!" calls the lad, rousing the darkness in her, "do you even know the way to whichever village you are taking us, or is it that you are lost?"

"Do you wish to witness how your beloveds are devoured, how their flesh bleeds and they cry and moan and groan 'til death sets them free?"

"How can you say such a thing, Arianna!"

"Do not waken the beasts, lad. I say, do not!"

"But I—"

"Be still," demand the others, walking on behind Arianna, who smiles her joy upon espying a pond, a pond in the grasp of the forest's vast plant life.

In the shade of the oldest of trees, the people kneel down and quench their thirst, while Arianna is watching them, awkwardly looking at each of them.

NOT FAR AWAY: For however long he had remained unwavering in his drive to find it, he has begun to lose hope a few days ago and has been ever since hinging the outcome of his search on luck.

From upon his horse he roams the forest with his eyes, looking back at the glade and the mountains beyond, behind which the Sun will soon begin to fall; and he looks at his companions—all mounted men armed with spears, swords and daggers—and says, "The day is almost over. We should spend the night in the glade. The horses must graze and rest—where could they better than here."

One of the horsemen dismounts and drives his spear into the ground, uttering loudly, "We are no more in the plain. Perhaps we should make a larger fire now to keep away whatever beings dwell here."

"No, we make several small fires around us. If anything happens, we can stand back to back." Nodding at his most trusted fellow, he says to him, "You and I are going to be the first on guard."

They set about preparing for the night, gathering wood and checking for snakes before they will let the horses graze. Though they believe that tonight is going to be a night alike others—which all of them treasure, for sitting in sight of the stars while talking about what may cause these orbs in the sky is the fortune of wanderers as 'tis of hunters—, they will soon realize how wrong they are.

When they have collected some wood and set ablaze torches, they bring the horses together, thereupon hearing a faint cry.

"What was that!" says one of them and advises each of his fellows to listen in a whisper, yet all the others perceive are the first yelps of beasts rousing from sleep.

"What did you hear?" his fellows ask him, looking at the horses to tell from their behavior whether danger is near.

"The horses are rather calm," says the leader. "Whatever you heard prowling about must not have been a beast of prey—"

"I heard a voice, someone's voice, not a beast on the prowl. I can still—listen!"

And they listen, hearing single voices shouting about, and thereupon these voices turn into a unified cry; and every mare and stallion begins to jitter at the squall.

"What is happening there!" shouts the leader, at once signing his fellows to mount. "Quick now!"

Though struggling with keeping their horses calm, they bestride their fine animals at once and ride into the forest, holding their troches aloft upon entering.

Alert
Though filled with joy upon seeing what his words of advice had brought about, worries preyed on his mind.

For several days Artias and his companions are now traveling straight across *the southern forest**. They march at a quick pace, although they dread to come across something unforeseen. The one night in Odas has proven just how many unknown things walk the Earth. Since then, Gordes and his fellows have been keeping their ears sharp and their eyes at all times focused on their surroundings. Nevertheless, the endless green around them, the trees growing to great height, the mountains, which would always strike them as infinite; the glades, the hills, the eternal beauty of the creatures' realm inspires them to find out more about these sacred grounds.

They come upon yet another glade, much greater than the ones before, as Artias tells everyone to stop and calls Gordes to him. Houses are seen at the far end of the glade, surrounded by a partly completed stockade.

"I visited that village once before," says he. "Maybe we are not the only ones going there. I must ask you, are you willing to follow me—come what may?"

"Yes, Artias—but say, why do you ask me this now? What have you discovered?"

"It could be that the people of Odas had gone to that village, and it could be that trouble awaits. If Hentario was right and people really do look upon me as a hero, then I should not have to justify myself, but if not, then you may not wish to be seen with me—"

"Enough," Gordes cries. "We will stand with you, come what may. We are companions now, and we are friends and brothers: we are men seeking the same, my kindred spirit."

Nodding shortly Artias heads on in the lead of the small group.

The first time he was in Veran the village had no stockade. Given that one is being erected now, the Elder of Veran must have understood what he had told him.

The closer he and his fellows draw, the more people emerge working on the stockade.

"They cut trees," Gordes says, amazed. "How did they manage to haul them, I wonder."

"Not all trees are as large as the ones we were ringed by," Artias says. "Oak trees, though large, are not as massive as a *Kandus*.*"

Whereas some of the villages in Arjovan are big, Veran isn't, but even so, to erect a stockade is a toil unlike any other. Trees must be felled, branches removed, and the bare trunks are then hauled from the forest to the village by horses and are eventually set upright into previously dug holes, a demanding task to erect but a single stake, especially for those who have not yet mastered this technique; nonetheless, the sheltering wall of wood is coming together—Veran is halfway bounded. Although many stakes are yet to be raised, they were prepared already. Artias is amazed at how skilled the people handle their axes and work together to built themselves a sheltering barrier against the peril of the night. With horses and ropes, tools and posts stake after stake is brought upright and secured in the earth.

When the hunter and his five companions arrive (treading carefully upon the planks carrying them across recently dug holes), the day draws to an end and the men and women who were working on the stockade are on their way home or to the tavern, while others take the horses to the stable.

"Let's head for the tavern," says Gordes, eager for a drink. "We must stay here 'til dawn anyway."

Hentario agrees, enjoying drinking as much as his fellow.

"A cup of wine will do us good," says Artias and advises everyone to drink within reason. "We might have a long way ahead of us."

"And where exactly will we go?" wonders Gordes.

"I must speak to Unelas first. He will certainly be able to tell me whether there are any other villages near his."

"I see, and who is Unelas?" asks Hentario.

"The Elder, head of Veran. Last time I have spoken to him, he told me of Odas, and I went on my way the next day."

"Let's go to Uneras, then," Gordes says shortly.

"His name is Unelas."

"Sounds the same to me."

"Well, it's not quite the same," says Hentario and spells the name of the Elder.

"Uneras, Unelas, where's the difference," grunts Gordes. "It's a funny name anyway."

"Is it?"

"Yes, or would you name your child like that? Uleras!"

"What the—are you doing this by purpose?" Artias draws a breath, saying that it's Unelas and not Uleras nor Uneras. "You might wish to simply address him by title rather than name."

"Why is that? I can say his name."

"Yes," Hentario mumbles, "we heard."

"All right, I said his name wrong, so what? As I said, it's a funny name anyway."

His fellows—among them Anjes, whose laughter grows Gordes' annoyance at the Elder's strange name—say, "It's but a name, and you can't say it."

"I can say it, and I did."

"Let us hear," says Anjes. "I mean, you can say my name, right?"

"Everyone can say your name—it's as common as my drinking habit."

"We should get moving," advises Artias. "I believe we all struggle with pronouncing names at times."

"Yes," Gordes grumbles, "especially with strange ones. Yes, strange, that's what it is."

Upon arriving at the tavern, Artias and his companions halt before the entrance and look around Veran. There are a few men with swords walking by, letting the group wonder whether these are the men who ought to bring down Artias.

"Trouble may await you mentioned," says Gordes, watching the men setting alight torch after torch along Veran's path, "but I doubt these men capable of taking us on all together."

"There shall be no blood," Artias states. "No one has to die."

"Until yet we do not know if they are looking for you," says Hentario.

"True," agrees Anjes. "They did not look at us, seemed rather carless of our coming."

With his thumb hocked into his belt whereto his sword's sheath is fastened, Gordes tells his fellows to be on guard. "Be prepared for the unforeseen."

"That would be for the best," Artias says and is about to step into the tavern as Gordes takes hold of his arm.

"The men who wish you harm, tell us how they look? If they are in the tavern, our fellows shall eavesdrop on any conversation they might have. That will let us know if they are planning something and give us an opinion of their nature."

"I cannot say who wrote the letter."

"So then let us know of someone you rememb—"

"Pointless. It might as well be that some of them could not make it here alive." Looking at his fellows, Artias tells them that it would be wiser to simply claim themselves worried travelers who have come by Odas sometime ago.

"If any one of them is here, they will raise their voices."

"Very well," utters Gordes and nods at his fellows to sign them to go and inquire before he leaves with Artias to wait nearby.

While waiting and observing the tavern's entrance with keen eyesight, Gordes asks his companion what he wishes to do if his worries happen to be reality. Artias takes a breath and shakes his head.

"If just I would have known what my wish to help had brought about. I am not even sure if I even could have helped the peopl—"

"Bah! You do good not to trouble yourself with such troublesome thoughts."

"True, yet I cannot."

"You might wish to try one day, then."

Before long Hentario emerges from the tavern, looking around for his friends while stepping from the porch upon Veran's path.

"Damn him," grunts Gordes, "he saw where we was going."

He is about to shout at his fellow to make known their position but keeps his strong voice at bay as Hentario descries them.

"Blind, are you?" says he, glaring at him. "You saw where we was going!"

"As you can see, Gordes, it's dark."

"Dark, yes, as dark as your eyesight."

"I say, calm yourself!"

"Say what you want, Hentario, say what you want! I see many torches glowing, so I do not care—"

"What is this!" Artias interrupts, fiercely staring at Gordes. "For what reason are you acting like this?"

Silence comes over all three men until Hentario defends Gordes by saying that he is simply tired, and he thereupon tells Artias, "We asked around about Odas, as you said, but nobody has been there recently. Appears to me like if they're all so busy with building the stockade, establishing rules, and forming groups to guard the village that they barely even noticed our arrival."

"What about the people of Odas?" asks Artias. "Perhaps they have been seen—"

"I am afraid not."

"But you said people barely even noticed—"

"I know what I said, but if they were here, we would have been told."

"Are you sure?"

"Artias, wherever they are, it is not here."

To hear this lets Artias shudder. He fears for every man and woman, every boy and girl of Odas; they should be here in Veran, unless they have been stumbling through the wilderness, knowing neither how to defend themselves if attacked by beasts nor how to tell which way to go ever since abandoning Odas.

Resolute to find and save whomever alive of these poor souls (who wanted to tie him to a tree to see whether the beast would take him), he asks Hentario to summon the others. "I have something to say."

"Now?" asks Gordes.

"Why don't we go to the tavern," says Hentario. "Our fellows are drinking just now, enjoying the safety of the walls around them—we should too."

"All right, I suppose I can speak to you in the tavern as good as anywhere."

"You can. Tables are too far apart as that anybody could eavesdrop. Speaking of that, your advice was worth gold."

"What advice?" asks Artias, wondered.

"That we shall claim ourselves travelers. Yes, Artias, you are a smart man. I am certain that you are as skilled with the bow as you are witted."

Wails

Where they were ... there unto them came a man who wished to tell them of the cries he had heard; he tried to help, as yet oblivious to the foulness that had taken place.

The tavern is small, crowded and emerges with good woodwork, fine tables, and a bar all along the wall facing the front door. Each wall is adorn with pictures of gatherings to display the strengths of Veran's community by showing unity.

Artias and the others—all formidable men, armed with bows and arrows, keen knives and swords—join their fellows at the bar. Anjes, Herjas, and Yorn have already ordered a bottle of dandelion wine and gladly ask the man behind the bar for three cups more.

Unlike Artias himself, his companions are used to drink spirits and are therefore, even when drinking two bottles of wine, never really drunk.

"You should not drink too much," Artias advises them, resolute to enjoy merely one cup of wine. "Your senses will be no more as they have been before."

"I do not worry about such things," Gordes mutters, gulping down the first cup and filling the next to the brim. "Wine never really manages to get me drunk. In fact, neither me nor my companions ever got drunk on wine—besides of you perhaps."

Approached by a man from behind, Artias cares little about saying anything to Gordes and heeds the sound of trudging steps.

"I heard you folks are travelers," says the man, looking at the group of sturdy built fellows. "I heard you were asking around about Odas."

Artias is the first to turn around to see who's talking to them. In sight of a man whose only friendly features are his eyes, he rises, asking, "You know anything about the events in Odas?"

"Events? Now that is a strong word for someone who claims not to know what happened."

"What is this about?"

Hearing the rough tone in the hunter's voice, Gordes and the others turn around, grimly looking at the man before them.

"I been working on the stockade the entire day," the man says. "Odas is quite the distance away, but I heard voices not so very long ago. These could have been made by a group of people, but not you, unless you hide children and women somewhere outside."

"What are you talking about?" asks Artias.

"The voices I heard sounded like women's and children's."

"I do not understand what you are saying?"

"Neither do I," says Gordes, getting up on his feet. "You say we are hiding women and children?"

"No, no, you misunderstand. I say—okay, listen here, I heard voices—"

"You said that," Hentario grunts angrily. "Now, what is it that you want to tell us?"

"A day before you arrived I heard people talking in the forest. I never go too close to the forest when it is in bloom but did to get some flowers for my wife. We had a fight, you see, and—ah, no matter. What I want to say is that I heard voices. Normally you do not hear voices talking so loudly among trees. You never know what might hear you. I thought it strange."

"Could you hear what these voices were saying?" asks Artias.

"No, I could not, and I was not eager to find out. I mean, who knows what might try to lure you in."

"No, no." Artias shakes his head, explaining that there are no beasts out there capable of Man's tongue. "But say, did it appear to you as if someone was in trouble?"

"I can't say. My ears are not so good, but as I said, they were talking loudly. Yes, yes, I'd even say anxiously."

"Where exactly was that?"

"South of here. There is a small carpet of flowers at the end of the glade."

"Have you told anybody?"

"Yes, I told Unelas, our Elder. He seemed to take the matter lightly."

"I know Unelas, spoke with him once," Artias says. "He did not seem to be a man who woul—"

"You were here before, right? Yes, yes, of course—I knew I know you from somewhere."

"Before you say another word, you should know that I think highly of Unelas."

"Hey, I am just saying how I see things."

"Good you do," says Hentario. "Perhaps that Elder of yours is a lazy one."

"No," Artias defends Unelas, with whom he spoke only once. "He took my advice serious, so I cannot imagine he woul—"

"Listen to me," the man utters fiercely. "If you do not believe me, go see him yourself and ask him about—"

"I did not say I do not believe you. I say Unelas might have known whose voices—"

"He told me, 'It certainly were traveling folks, tribes.' There are many of these. Yes. Arjovan. Our Sun, our home. People come and come, so I thought he might be right, but if not—I just think he should have looked into it."

"Your words confuse me," Gordes grunts. "You speak of one things and then of something else."

"You want me to get you some flowers, too?"

"Yes, you may get me flowers. I wish to have flowers, so go, go and get me some. Tread out into the dark and get me some flowers. Perhaps I will be the one who hears your voice crying out then, and I shall be as deaf and cowardice as you—"

"Enough of this," Artias shouts and looks at the man. "Thank you for telling me."

"I though I should."

"Say, have you noticed anything strange ever since?"

"Ever since what?"

Hentario shakes his head, muttering, "You are not very bright, are you?"

Thumping the bar with his first, Artias glares at Hentario as if demanding him to watch his mouth, and he then tells the man: "Have you noticed anything peculiar since you had heard these voices you told me of."

"No, nothing."

"Okay, I shall speak to Unelas later on; and, yes, I—*we*—will look into this."

"No, no, I am not going anywhere with you. My wife, she doesn't like to be home alone."

"Well, actually, I meant me and my companions."

"Oh, yes, sure, of course, yes—I... I go and finish my drink now, yes?"

"Of course."

Watching the man returning to his table, Artias ponders over what he said for an instant and thereupon tells his companions that he will make his way to the Elder's house now.

"In the middle of the night?" asks Yorn.

"The nigh is yet young, my fellow."

Artias drinks his cup empty at once and leaves the tavern, looking around the village in search of Unelas' house.

"Where was it," he wonders, treading along the path towards the stockade.

Soon it dawns on him that the Elder lives at the rear of Veran, where the stockade does not reach to yet.

"How annoying," he mutters and stops in his tracks and walks back the whole way, past the stockade and the tavern to a small house with two chimneys. He sees light shining out into the night from one of the windows and raises his hand to knock as the door opens and Unelas, a bald man of great age, steps out.

"Artias," says he, confused to see him in front of his house. "I did not expect to see you again so soon—how do you like the stockade?"

"I am glad you took my advice."

"You seemed to know what you talk about. Besides, I believe precaution is the best caution."

"I need to speak to you, Unelas."

"Now? I was just about to leave for a drink. How about you join me and—"

"I am afraid it allows no delay."

A little worried about the unknown, Unelas remains still for an instant.

"Well, if it is so important, then you better come in." Stepping back into his house, the Elder asks Artias whether he would like something to drink.

"I just had a cup of wine."

"I am not offering you wine. I was going to offer you ale."

"I am fine as I am."

Looking around at the well-made furnitures arranged neatly and in order and at all the nicely decorated window frames adding much to the already beautiful interior of this small house, he must say, "You have a nice home. I did not remember it being so... warm."

"I do my best, thank you. But say, what about did you want to talk to me?"

"I was told of voices that had been heard in the surrounding forest?"

"Voices... yes, Alarion told me of them. He said he heard the voices of men, women, and children—is it this you are worried about?"

"Are you not?"

"Well, it is as I told him: There are many traveling tribes that wander this land in search of a place to settle. I am sure that what he heard there were folks talking and arguing about which way to go."

"Did you look into this, or have you—"

"Look into it? Artias, the stockade needs our full attention—*my* full attention. I could not just sent someone into the forest to find out what could have been going on. We are neither warriors nor fighters who can relay on the sword to keep them safe. Honest, hardworking men we are, Artias."

"I understand."

"Do you really, because the way you look at me isn't exactly friendly. You glare at me, so forgive me if I do not quite believe you. If you think my decision was foolish, say so!"

"I wouldn't say foolish, Unelas. Say, did—"

"Then what? Perhaps idiotic, or better even, made without thought?"

"You took my advice, which shows that you, as the Elder of Veran, care about your people—"

"Of course I do!"

"And because you do, Unelas, because you do you should have at least tried to make sure that these voice have not been uttered by dying souls!"

"What do you mean by 'dying souls'?"

"People in distress, honest and hardworking folks in peril. If they were in distress, Veran could have been—or may still be—in danger. As you know, not everyone who comes to Arjovan is a man of peace and honor. No, Unelas, some are foul, wicked, and sinful in nature, seeking only to feed their own desires."

"You speak of bandits?"

"I speak of those to whom the lives of others are a mere possession to be owned. Now, I must know, Unelas, did you hear screams?"

"No, I did not hear anything. After Alarion had told me about voices, I went out and spent a while heeding every noise I could heard. No human sound reached my hearing, Artias—say, do you assume we are at risk?"

"I do not know. Fear not, though, because me and my companions, we shall find out whether you are, and we will find out what happened."

"These people, could they have been attacked by the claws of the forest?"

"The claws of the forest?" wonders Artias.

"All the meat-eaters out there."

"Ah, I see. I cannot say what took place yet. Maybe yes, maybe no. It may as well be as you told Alarion, but precaution is the best caution."

"Indeed."

"Say, Unelas, did you see anyone from Odas?"

"Odas? Do you think the voices—"

"Could have been the people of Odas."

"Alarion may not seem to be the brightest man on earth, but he is no liar—never was. I believed him yet heard nothing myself." Unelas paces up and down, wondering if his decision was the right one and trying to look upon himself as a good leader. "But if someone was in peril, then I failed to be what I ought to be."

"We will find out the truth," says Artias, honest as ever in his intentions. "We will leave by dawn, and until then make sure that you have men watching the night, and make sure that no one leaves alone."

"I made rules regarding the night and chose strong men for guards."

"A wise decision indeed. Veran is among the first villages with guards, and soon you will also have a stockade, and then, my friend, then life will be much less of a danger."

"I was thinking about building a hall once the stockade is complete."

"A hall?"

"Yes, a town hall where I can assemble everyone and publicly announce my decisions, giving my people the chance to speak their doubts then and there."

"That is a marvelous idea."

"Thank you. I will certainly help building it. If you look at my furnitures, you will see what a good woodworker I am."

"You made all of them?"

The furnitures are truly well-made and adorn with engraved silhouettes of horses or birds on the wing.

"Yes, I did."

"What is your trade?"

"As you know, I am an Elder."

"And before?"

"What shall I say, I used to fix people's furnitures for little gold. That was until I came here to Arjovan. Many years have gone by since then, I can tell you."

"I see. I should be returning to my companions now. Perhaps we won't be seeing each other again until to our return, in which case I hope that we will have good news in our bags."

"Do you need equipment or supplies? Perhaps both?"

"Do not worry, all I need I have. The creatures' realm, it is not mine to live in but provides me with all my needs nevertheless."

A knock on the door silences the discussion, and worries arouse when it turns to heavy banging.

"Elder Unelas!" someone calls from beyond the door, pounding it further. "Open up!"

Artias forthwith hustles to the door, opening it at once, and a slender fellow with shaking hands and a pale faces dashes in, uttering anxiously, "There's trouble in the tavern!"

Tribulation
Unaware of the event that was to follow their arrival, they soon found themselves confronted with armed men and endeavored to keep the peace and be just unto their adversaries.

There is no telling what is happening in tavern from outside: the night is dark and still, allowing not a thought on what is taking place there. But upon entering the tavern, blood catches Artias' sight, and the body of a man lies before Gordes' feet.

"What is going on," cries he, engulfed by the eyes of all the people near him, who dare not rise from their chairs.

Gordes looks down at the corpse of a man he killed with many thrusts and says that this one had come to harm his fellow.

"What are you talking about?"

Several men come dashing into the tavern, holding swords in their hands and bows raised, held ready to fire as they demand everyone to stand still.

"What happened," they shout at Artias, shoving him over to Gordes. "You arrived with them, yes? Foul men you are!"

"No," yells Gordes but is told to hush thereupon.

"I WILL NOT," he shouts, pointing at the dead man before him. "HE WANTED TO HARM MY FELLOW."

The group of men tell everyone to stay sitting, and then they look at Gordes with raised bows and tell him to hold close his mouth and let fall that knife in his hand, "Or you will be brought down."

Artias, though amazed at how these men come forth, even though they have yet been declared guards, says that they shall heed what Gordes has to say for the truth to be unraveled.

"Let him speak," says he. "Let him explain!"

Seeing Unelas joining the group, he tells him that his guards must allow Gordes to have his say. "Hear him out."

"A murder," Unelas stutters, "a murder." He cannot believe that a murder took place here in Veran where not a soul ever turns against the other.

"HOW DARE YOU, HOW DARE YOU DEFEND A MURDERER," he shouts at Artias.

"You must know what happened before claiming him the attacker, Elder—you must to be just."

"He came to harm my fellow," Gordes repeats, and when he is then told to state what took place, he says that this man he stabbed down had come to him asking about Artias.

"He said he wanted to know where the hunter is. He said he saw him arriving here with us and that we should tell him where he is."

"He just attacked," says Hentario. "Gordes had to defend his life."

In silence Unelas treads towards the corpse, wondering who that was—he has never seen him before. After a mere moment he sends all the people expect for the barman home, ordering everyone to stay at home and lock their doors.

Not one of the guards says a word 'til folks have left and they are alone among their Elder and the men whom they deem villains.

"Shall we send them away without weapons and clothes?" they ask Unelas, "or shall we imprison them?"

"TRY TO," Gordes shouts, taking a step forwards.

"Stop where you stand," says Artias, seizing his friend by the arm. "Let me speak."

"There is nothing to say," declares Unelas. "Not a word is to be said."

"This is wrong." Yorn gradually raises his voice. "You cannot and shall not do this!"

"SILENCE!" Unelas is furious and guided only by his ire and abhorrence, yet he listens to Artias who says that the one who holds someone's fate in hands must be willing to deal with both parties without threatening the integrity of either one.

"Let your friend speak, then," Unelas says.

Gordes steps forth, claiming the man he slew a rogue whose aim was clear.

"And what was his aim?" asks Unelas, saying further that he shall choose his words with caution.

"He wanted to kill my fellow. Yes, he wanted to—I saw it in his eyes, by the way he spoke of Artias, by the way he looked as he spoke of Artias. Even before h—"

"He was foul," Hentario interrupts, "asking us about our companion in a way that left no doubt of his motive."

Unelas takes another look at the dead body and asks the guards if they have seen this man before.

"Yes," one of them says, "he had arrived upon a horse shortly before we were alerted of a fight here."

"By whom?"

"Alarion summoned us, came running to us, telling us of a fight, saying someone might get killed. We were too late as you can see."

"Did you speak to the victim before he entered the tavern?"

"Only to request that he leave his spear with his horse. He assured us he would. He was very polite."

"That alone does not make a good man," shouts Anjes. "A kind word alone means nothing—a man's deeds tell his character!"

"What brought about the fight?" Artias asks Gordes, hoping his answer will not cause his downfall.

"He told me that he will slice your throat."

"He just told you that." Unelas shakes his head and approaches Gordes at once. "Why would he tell you that? Why would he make known in front of everyone that he is about to kill someone?"

"I did not trust him, so I said I was looking for Artias on someone's behalf. I told him that he must wait 'til we have dealt with him, and he asked me how we intend to deal with him, and I said we are going to kill him. Thereupon he said that he is to slice his throat and no one else—ask whomever was in the tavern before. Go and ask them and they will tell you what I just told you."

"What happened then?" Artias asks. "Did he attack you?"

"Yes, he did. I said I lied and that I am your friend, and he pulled a dagger. He tried to do so without me seeing it, but I did see the blade. Yes, I did see the blade. He realized that I had seen it and tried to stab me down. Too slow. I was quicker."

It is more than difficult for Unelas to think of something to say; he never had to deal with (such) a murder before and doesn't quite know what to do besides of telling his guards to drive off the group. However, he asks Artias for his opinion on the situation.

"The people of Odas," says Artias, "they wrote a letter in which they claimed me the reason for their leaving. They say I am to blame for the coming of a beast."

"What are you talking about, Artias?"

"I tried to help the people of Odas deal with the claws of the forest. I was there for the same reason that had brought me to Veran. They already had problems with—listen to me, Unelas, I tried to help them, but it might be that they wish me gone now. They turned against me, forcing my hand against them."

Unelas, though often capable of keeping his (true) feelings a secret, cannot hide his fears from showing, and with a trembling voice he asks suspiciously, "Are you saying that you had quarrel in Odas?"

"More than—"

"Listen very carefully, Artias. I am grateful for all the advice you have given me already; nevertheless, I do not want to hear of any of your doings in the past. Whatever was in Odas is not on me to judge. Veran concerns me only and nothing else shall, and now I ask you to leave. You all leave now as you emerge before me."

"How dare you!" Gordes utters fiercely. "We have done you no wrong—ask the barman, damn it." Looking at the bartender, he says that he shall tell them what happened. "You know I speak the truth, the whole truth, and nothing but the truth."

Though the barman nods (knowing that no lie was told), Unelas says, "You killed a man, a man I do not know and therefore cannot vouch for. It happened here in Veran, however, which is why you can consider my demand a merciful one. You may thank Faron, the barman, for that."

"You do not want to ask Faron anything?" Gordes cannot believe how quickly he and his fellows are banished from Veran, although they did not start the fight and sought none either, and even if Artias says that the bartender can tell him everything and that he must listen to him like he listened to Gordes, Unelas merely says: "I wanted him to stay so that he can tell me what he had witnessed, and his nod has already told me what I must know; and you, you shall know that I do not banish you out of spite but for the well-being of my people."

Unelas considers banishment as the only way to deal with Gordes and his companions without needing to fight him and his sturdy fellows just because they actually should be slain all together. To Artias it seems as if the Elder's judgment is clouded and his verdict on the situation blinded by the sight of the blood reddening the ground.

Fuming with anger he and his five companions leave the tavern, trudging away into the darkness embracing Veran. Anger is strong in each of the six men, and they look back at the village with contempt and revulsion.

"A barking dog he was," Hentario comments shortly, striding with his fellows through the dead of night.

"We should go no farther," advises Artias. "It is too dangerous to walk around at night."

"He wants us dead." Gordes turns around, shouting at the Elder from the distance: "YOU WANT US DEAD, SO YOU SENT US AWAY, OUT INTO THE NIGHT. YOU LACK THE COURAGE TO KILL US YOURSELF. LETTING THE BEASTS DEAL WITH US, THAT

IS THE DOINGS OF A COWARD. A DAM—"

"BE STILL," Artias demands. "The wilds have ears."

"Let the beasts come, let them attack us, prey on us, or try to drag us to wherever they want to feast on us!"

"You want to die?" asks Hentario. "I do not want to be devoured and I am sure Anjes, Yorn, Herjas, and Artias do not wish so either, so hush your mouth."

Silence takes hold of everyone, and they wait and wonder where to go while all around them the sound of the night robs them their breath, and they hear growls and yelps and roars joining in howls.

"Where shall we go?" Yorn wonders. "Where shall we go? Gordes, tell us where to go? You lead us, so decide for us; or you, Artias, say what we—"

"I say we go back," utters Gordes, "and let them see and feel the injustice that took place."

"No," says Artias. "We wait, stay wary and vigilant 'til day's first light."

None of them can distinguish anything more than the face of the night, this endless gloom 'neath the sky that robs their sights. They believe to see things moving about, claim to have seen the eyes of the beasts lurking about. And they say, "Whatever critter may come upon us shall find us standing in grim defense, willing to fight to the very end"; and they cry, "To our dying day we remain steadfast!" And they muster their courage and draw closer together, above all fearing to have their flesh torn off to the bone beneath.

Engulfed in darkness they stand, swearing at the Elder's lack of sense with every noise the night brings forth, and they say that he is a fool, and they tell each other that he has never raised arms, for he would not have been so abhorred of the blood if he had.

"I though wisdom comes with age," says Hentario, "appears, it does not."

Unlike the others Artias stays quiet; every word he says distracts him for longer than he can afford. Shapes caused by his own imagination come into being darker than the gloom embracing him and his allies, floating through the air or moving unnaturally through the blackness. The sound of the night with all the inhuman cries coming with it lets his fears come to life, manifested in shapes; and every time he believes to see something, he feeds his fright.

"We cannot stay in the open," he tells his fellows, saying thereupon that they shall follow him.

The faint touch of light from every torch shining in Veran guides him the way back. Gordes believes that the hunter is up to showing the Elder that he is not to be trifled with.

Once they stand before Unelas' house and Artias knocks to see whether the Elder is home, Gordes asks why he does not simply enter to make known to the Elder that he better rethink the penalty. Artias looks around quickly before entering the house, signing his fellows to come along silently, and he then says that he does not intent to do anything else than wait for sunrise.

"You just broke in," Hentario states. "Do you really think he'll just let us wait in his house after he banished us."

"No, but when he comes back, I shall ask him to grant us a stay for the night."

"You think he's still in the tavern?"

"Well, nobody is home. Besides, the front door was open, so, yes, he may still be in the tavern, dealing with the body alongside of his guards."

"Maybe he's home and simply forgot to put the batten," says Yorn.

"If so, he would be here, which he isn't. I knocked, you remember."

Bursting with rage, Gordes draws his blade and strikes a dent into the frame of a bookcase with the pommel.

"Solid oak," grunts he. "I should use his head to break his furniture."

"Stop this!" demands Artias. "As long as you travel with me you shall neither commit vandalism nor hurt anyone."

"I tell you what I am going to do, Artias. I will go to the stable, get myself the spear of my foe, and urge it all through Uneras, Unea—however his name."

"The stable is too close to the tavern," says Yorn. "You will be seen."

"Whoever sees me will know me as their nemesis forth on!"

"I will stop you if need be," utters Artias, approaching his fellow. "You shall not come off you way, Gordes. I beg of you, do not make me stop you."

"He sent us to die in the wilderness, Artias!"

"I know."

"If you know, then act, or I will!"

"You wished to join me, Gordes, all of you did; and now that you have, do not forget why you had wanted to."

THE ELDER'S RETURN: Before long Unelas is on his way home, as yet not knowing of his visitors.

Finding out what to do with the body to avert creatures from following the odor of dead flesh was difficult, allowing no other way than to besprinkle the corpse with salt and put it down into the cellar of the tavern until it can be buried. After doing that, the desire to go home was greater than ever before.

By the moment he opens the door, he is seized by the arm and torn into his own house. He fears for his life and rages around to free himself from whomever's grasp he's in.

"OFF WITH YOU," he shouts, cursing whoever holds him until Gordes emerges, showing him the shining blade of his sword.

"Stop shouting," says Artias, astonishing the Elder by his presence.

"What are you doing here?" Unelas stutters, assuming Artias seeks vengeance. "Did you chose to become a burglar, willing to prey on an old man and kill him?"

"You know me better than to assume something like that."

"Then what do you want?"

"A place to spend the night."

"Ah, I see, you think breaking in makes that possible."

"As you see, it did," Gordes utters angrily, waving the sword around the Elder's face, "or do you think otherwise?"

He signs Hentario to let go off the Elder and shove him away from the door.

Staggering by the hard push, Unelas falls in front of Artias' feet, feeling as if the hunter takes joy in his humiliating position.

"You like to look down on an old man, Artias—I thought better of you!"

"You may rise anytime you like, Unelas. I am not here to hurt you or do you wrong, but you must understand the reason for my en—"

"The reason for you breaking into my house is your drive for vengeance, isn't it?"

"No, Unelas, no! Listen, we need a place to spend the night, and we both know that your punishment wasn't made with thought, so grant us this wish and we shall leave at dawn."

"You leave me no choice than to grant you your wish."

"Tell us to leave and we shall forthwith," Artias says, much to his fellows' displeasure. "Before you do so, however, let me ask you if you do look upon me as a burglar or as the man who came to you only to help you live a safer life."

"Safer? I do not feel safe, Artias."

"You banished us. Is banishment at night not almost the same as killing us?"

Unelas must admit, "Yes, it is."

He did not know what his penalty actually meant for Gordes and his companions. Though he spoke with the bartender and a few others who had witnessed the fight and eventually struck upon the understanding that Gordes should not have been blamed, he dared not to go after them, struggled to even call after them. This, at least, is what Artias assumes.

"What do you want to hear, Artias? That I done wrong? Fine, I did not treat—"

"Grant us a stay for the night and you will see neither me nor my companions anymore."

"Listen to me, the banishment, I cannot simply let that be forgotten. I would lose my face and my people's faith in me—it is difficult."

"So?" grunts Gordes. "I'll gladly never return when day's first light allows me to depart from these unjust grounds of yours."

Unelas rise to his feet and looks at Artias.

"If you could tell me whether the voices—"

"I will look into that matter, as I told you, and I shall only return if danger is to be assumed."

Yorn, whose anger at the Elder grows steadily, wishes to show Unelas just how greatly he loathes him for his decision by claiming all the ale and wine he may find in this house his fellows' belonging. But robbery is not something Artias wants to take part in and neither allows his companions to.

"We are honorable men," says he. "You chose to follow me, so act as the brave men that you are."

"People like him make it hard for us to be brave," Herjas comments shortly, sitting down upon a small stool near the door. "They make it hard for us to not come off our way again. I say, Elder, there were days, I can tell you, oh, what would I have done to you!"

Janderas
Nothing could be said to awaken their foes to the truth, but whereas blood would not tell, a tongue could.

When the day dawns, Artias speaks not a word with Unelas and leaves with his five companions as he said he would. He leaves Veran quickly and marches south, approaching the forest in hopes of finding the carpet of flowers Alarion mentioned.

"Are you sure we're going the right way?" Gordes asks.

"Yes. Alarion said 'to the south', so south is where I am goi—"

"Wait, what are you talking about?"

"The voices Alarion heard—"

"Is that what you told the Elder you will look into?"

"Yes."

"Why?"

"Because that is what I do."

"You mean, that's what *we* do."

"Yes."

"You should have told us."

"You knew I was going to look into it—you know since we were drinking in the tavern."

"That's right," says Hentario. "You told the halfwit that you'll—"

"You should not speak of people like that."

"He was a halfwit!"

"His name was Alarion, and I wish that you refer to him by his name only."

"Fine, you told Alarion you'll look into it, but I must say, you might as well could have meant that you'll look into the reason for the Elder's laziness, which is more than clear to us now—he's simply an idiot and a fool."

"A foolish idiot," remarks Herjas.

"Whatever he is," Gordes utters, "I did not know that we decided to—ah, it matters not. At least we have something to do, right?"

In sight of the trees growing larger and higher at their every step, Artias tells his fellows to look out for flowers.

"A carpet of flowers he said," Hentario mentions, roaming his eyes over the glade.

"There," he tells the others, pointing at many violet flowers coloring the greenery of the glade.

Watchfully they stride towards the forest, staying close by the flowers 'til trees surround them. Artias stops in his tracks and inspects the ground beneath his feet and the vegetation around.

"Many creatures passed by, but I see no tracks made by people. There is not a trace that tells of someone's passing."

All the paths worn into the ground were made by beings other than humans; nevertheless, Artias discovers something of interest: one of the sticks he made in Odas. With amazement he raises the spear, showing it to his fellows and saying that he made this one among six others in Odas.

"So what is it dong here?" Gordes wonders.

"The tip, the stick's tip shows blood," says Anjes.

The entire pointed end is covered with dry blood. It appears, the spear has been thrown at something quite a while ago.

"What is out there lurking about," murmurs Gordes, keenly staring into the green as if something caught his eye. Through the vegetation he then descries creatures with four legs and great necks, and the ground trembles slightly when he wants to tell his fellows that something is coming at them. Before he can utter a word, seven horsemen emerge from behind the foliage. The spears they carry—fine spears with sharp blades and adorn shafts—are held at the group as they dismount their fine animals and drive Artias and his fellows together.

"Beast speaker," they call the hunter, demanding him to step forth.

Amid the ten horsemen is one whose spear has myriads of short leather strings tied to its shaft. "One for each I killed," says he.

"What is the meaning of this?" shouts Gordes. "Who are you?"

The man cares not to answer and glares at Artias, saying with a menacing tone of voice, "Why is that you sent the people of Odas to die in exile?"

"What? I did not do anything like that!"

"No? I heard something else. I was told that you speak with beasts, making pacts with these and earning your gold by driving off whatever creature you let loose upon the people you claim to help." The man slams his hand against his chest, letting the metal rings that form his armor ring. "I shall drive you off this land, beast speaker."

"I tried to help them!"

"You caused their fellows' deaths."

"No, I... I tried to help them. I did try to help them, but that man, that foul man made every soul turn against me!"

"That is not true. I spoke with everyone, making sure that I track the right one."

"What are you saying? Tell me, what is going on here? On whose behalf are you—"

"We went to their aid when we heard their screams. They called each other, cried out into the night that a creature is after them. It emerged, but with a spear in its flesh it ran back to where it had come from. There came more, more creatures that we—me and my men—had to fight off to save these people, those you had wished to see dead."

"Where are they now?"

"Why? Do you desire vengeance? I can see that you do, so do not lie to me!"

"I merely wish to know if they are safe."

"I brought them back to the place you had sent them away from, assuring them that the beast speaker will be brought to justice for his doings. You face me now, Artias."

All of the horsemen appear skilled and strong, capable of wielding their weapons unlike anyone else. Gordes and his men, no matter their endurance and resilience, cannot compete with these riders.

"Who are you?" asks Hentario; yet he is told to be still, "or lie dead on the ground".

"Enough of this!" shouts Artias. "I killed three men in rage, all of whom were from Odas; but I had come to them only to help them, to make them see the danger around them. The divine one forgave me my sins, allowing me to continue the path I walk."

"I shall not heed the words of a murderer."

"To be just you must!"

"Dare you claim me a scoundrel!"

"You are if you do not listen. All that I do, I do to help."

"If so, then what with these men you killed? Gilgaron, Tindras, Beras, Ardega—"

"Ardegan dashed into the darkness, unwilling to listen to me. I called him, shouted at him to return. He did not listen!"

"There are yet three more whose deaths you brought by."

"I did kill Gilgaron, and I did kill Tindras and Beras. There is nothing to say about that. I did it, and that is that. Before you cannot hold back your desire to strike any longer, tell me where you met the people of Odas."

"Lost in this wilderness, not far from where you will be put to rest."

"A fool's talk," Hentario shouts. "How foolish of you to bring them back to Odas rather than to Veran. Yes, horsemen, Veran would have been closer, but you could not see, because you do not know this forest. You are lost in your thoughts and far off your way. You ride on horses, because your legs are weak; and you hold spears, because you do not dare to face your foe up close; and you use men to do your trade, because you're too stupid to find your way—you are an insult to yourself!"

"Appears, the one with the biggest mouth is to fall first." The man thrusts his spear into the ground and draws a sword, demanding that Hentario unsheathe his.

"No," cries Artias, rushing between them. "How much more blood will it take 'til you realize that we seek the same?"

"As much as it takes to have this land be seen as the place where the wicked souls are brought to the sword."

"And yet you act wicked, caring little about what we have to say as you act blinded by your favor for the people of Odas, people I have tried to help."

"Then speak of the event that caused you to be seen a—"

"No, no more I will. If you want to attack me, then do so, but my companions shall take no part in our fight—they have nothing to do with this."

"One question, let it be one question that will decide whether you live or die."

"One question?"

"Yes."

"So then, let me hear your question."

"Are you willing to return to Odas with me and listen to the people's accusations?"

"Yes, yes I am willing, and that not only to see if they are well."

"Good. Your companions, they must join—"

"No," Gordes utters furiously, outraged at the leader's behavior.

"You are not the one to tell me what I am to do and what not! We stand with Artias, though, so we will accompany him come what may."

"Searching for trouble, are you?"

Gordes is, above all, cautious: the fellow he slew in the tavern bore a spear and rode a horse, as stated by the guards. Perhaps he belonged to these horsemen.

"I follow whom I trust," says he. "Your barking is not the reason why we are coming along—Artias is."

"You do not have a choice!"

"I will have you apologize for injustice," utters Gordes.

"Injustice? You will be thrust to death anytime soon now."

"This is just about enough!" yells Artias, glaring at the leader. "Say, what brought you here to this forest anyway?"

"We hunt villains, because that is what we do, and that is what we do best."

"You have horses and hunt villains, so tell me, do you hunt in the northern plain?"

"Why is that of interest to you?"

"Because my kin hunt villains, too!"

"Your kin?"
"Yes."
"And they are?"
"Tanara, Hervjol, Hjos—"
"Tanara? You say Tanara is your kin?"
"She is my sister."
"I find that hard to believe."
"It seems you prefer to believe strictly what you feel like."
"Tanara killed Vartos—that foul villain—and many of his vile men. She slew those who lingered around the plain before I fist met her—"
"Do not try to trick me, horsemen. Tanara did not kill Vartos, Hervjol did. And, if you are who you say you are, you know as good as I that bandits dwell in caves on the mountains. Speak now, what were you doing here?"
"We should move now, Artias," says the leader, sheathing his blade upon grasping his spear. "On the way, I might tell you what I strive to find, unless it turns out that you are not related to Hjos, Hervjol, or Tanara, my wife."

The horsemen walk beside their horses, guiding their animals through the greenwood on foot while heeding every noise that might be made by the claws of the forest.

Throughout the day Artias observes their leader, wondering whether he truly is his sister's husband. He has not seen Tanara for years, so he cannot be sure. In truth, he saw his kindred last when he parted for his undertaking, and this he tells the leader of the horsemen, asking him thereupon, "Does my sister still wield the sword of our father?"

"She never owned a sword, beast speaker. She dislikes to fight with anything heavier than a knife!"

"That is true."

"Then why do you ask me—ah, I see, you test me, try to find out if my words are the truth. I tell you, Artias, Tanara does not speak much about her brother, so tell me, tell me how likely it is that I believe anything you say?"

"We parted ways long ago."

"She spoke only once of her brother. He abandoned us is what she said."

"She would never say that! My aim is brave she said when our paths separated! All of my kin think highly of my doing. Not one there is who would disapprove."

The leader hushes and thinks back on the days as he spoke with his wife about her brother. She told him that he wanders the land to help the people and said that his heart is golden and his thoughts deep. But what she said that could let him see Artias as her brother is the fact that the hunter's name has a meaning for which to tell one must be able to speak Nahess. Though he himself cannot speak this tongue (for it is utterly complicated), he knows the meaning of Artias.

Ordeal

They faced the greatest beasts of prey, fighting with spear(s) and sword(s) against the horde, with courage facing the ordeal of the attack—an act of valor, but even so, lives were lost.

"Your name has a meaning, right?" the leader of the horsemen inquires of Artias, looking at him as if he say: you better not lie about this.

Artias shrugs, saying merely, "Many names do."

"So what is the meaning of yours?"

"E am art Ias."

"I do not speak Nahess."

"I said I am a-giver."

"A-giver?"

"In Nahess a-giver is a person who assist others by giving them something such as help or advice."

"Nahess appears to be a dying language, giver."

"It is a-giver. Being called giver would mean I am a trader."

"Seems it is a complicated language, too."

"At times I think so myself."

After a moment of silence, the leader introduces himself as Janderas, "husband of your sister."

"So you believe me now?"

"I do, my fellow. You correctly answered everything that I had asked you, so why shall I doubt."

"Now we suddenly are your friends, huh?" Gordes grumbles and raises his voice, shouting: "I say, there are but a few who can tame a wild horse. Tell me, horsemen, are you missing one of your own!"

"Are you trying to tell me something. If so, then you better mind you—"

"You commanded someone to kill the brother of your wife! Such a command tells a lot about your character—a doubtful one you have."

Janderas shakes his head, saying that he very well knows who killed his friend.

"Many eyes saw you doing it," says he. "But as many eyes saw that you had no fault. Perjn, he always was—"

"Who are you talking about?" Hentario asks, wondered.

"The man your friend killed, his name was Perjn."

"So he was sent by you!" Herjas utters angrily.

"Indeed."

"And now he is dead. I guess that did not turn out quite as you had hoped."

"Greed ended his life!"

"Why would you say that?" wonders Artias.

"Because it is the truth."

"He betrayed us," says one of the other horsemen, a strong fellow who has married into Artias' kinsfolk sometime ago. "If we had not hunted you, we might have never seen through to his core. I nevertheless ask you to forgive me for wishing to kill whose aunt I have married. I speak for as all when I asks you to forgiv—"

"At least introduce yourself," says Yorn. "Whoever of you is somehow related to Artias shall introduce himself."

"Very well, I am Werhanjo and—"

"I say," utters Gordes, "was Perjn related to Artias, too? Was he?" At once staring at Artias, he continues, saying: "I would not have killed him if so—I shall not raise my hand against my fellow's kin!"

"Perjn was perfidious," shouts Janderas, raising his spear. Enraged at his fellow's breach of trust, he glares at its blade, saying that he would carve it with his fellow's name and spear Perjn's heart if he would not have been slain already.

"I told him to ride to the nearest village after we escorted everyone back to Odas," says he. "I told him to come back to me, commanded that he come back to me upon finding out if the beast speaker be there—I say, Artias, I did not know whom I wished to slay and was eager to cut you down for both your doings in Odas and for claiming the name of my wife's brother."

"But why," says Hentario, "why do you say your companion betrayed you?"

"I said he shall gallop to Veran. 'Veran,' I said, 'gallop there and stop only when you must.' He should have come to us not long after we had reached the glade. We all had seen Veran during our search and knew that he, as the skilled rider he was, must have arrived there a day before we even reached the glade. He did not return.

I asked my most trusted fellow to find out what had taken place. We feared he might have been taken by the forest. But, no, that he was not. What Werhanjo found out could only abhorred me. I was disgusted ... to my very core I felt but loathing. We are righteous men, never betraying each other. Perjn's greed killed him. The desire to let the people of Odas pay him for slaying Artias killed him, and I—"

Janderas hits hard upon soil and rock at a tug of his beloved horse. Pulled through the dirt 'til he lets off the rein, he cries, "What is going on", upon rising with drawn blade.

The other horses shy and snort before they bolt, following the one that has run off already.

But a step farther left and Janderas would be knocked over by mares and stallions, which would crush him beneath their hooves; he would be left to wait for death with broken bones and mashed organs, though a fate no act of fortune could avert should befall the whole of the group, for there before them they see what can only be one of the greatest of predators; and for however long they look at this shape within the green all around them, they can tell that there lurks no lonesome critter but a pack.

"It moves not," says Janderas, feeling the many eyes that are set upon them yet only able to gawk at the critter before them, of which everyone can see but its fur, for the rest is cloaked in leafage. He believes to see a hound-like beast with large curved claws, saying, "Wolves" to his fellows, though they say, "No wolf has crimson fur."

"It lies in wait," Gordes whispers to Artias, who cries at everyone he is among that they are about to be attacked.

"Be ready!" shouts Janderas, all at once witnessing the first beast vaulting through the green at one of his fellows, straight tearing his companion away into the forest.

"WERHANJO!" he cries, about to charge headlong after the beast.

Seizing him by the arm, Artias tears him to a halt.

"THERE ARE MORE AROUND!" he yells at him. "WE NEED YOUR SWORD, JANDERAS!"

"I MUST SAVE HIM!"

"HE IS GONE—GONE!"

"NO, HE IS—"

"STAND STEADFAST!" Gordes commands.

He and his men are ready to face whatever else may come to drag them away. With grim courage they stand ready to fight, and with swords and bows held firmly in their grasp, they—who do not fear to die, not now nor ever—cry at every beast near or far, "DARE COME AND YOU BE SLAIN"; and the beasts dare. They come dashing out of the greenery in hordes, seizing and tearing man after man away from the group: they strike not once at their prey, merely seize hold of them on their way through to devour each catch away from the group before they emerge anew.

The cries of those who feel the beasts biting their way through the armor to the flesh underneath is to their fellows as if a dagger pierce their hearts. While the begs and screams of the fallen carry on in the minds of ever soul trying to survive, the light breaching the darkness of their ordeal begins to fade. The creatures they try to fight off, critters born to hunt by far more effectively than them, are too fast as that they could ward their own: no sword, sharp enough; no strike, quick enough—they can't but hope that the beasts withdraw as long as a few of them still stand.

Hentario and Gordes witness their friends' endeavors to get free of the claws by which they are held and pledge to slay every beast that joins the feast.

"WE SHALL NOT YIELD," they vow; and "NOT EVER SHALL WE FALL," they say; "WE STAND TALL (and) NOT EVER WILL WE FALL."

And they challenge every critter arising from the greenery; and they thrust at these beasts' legs and aim for a strike at their necks, and they shout at their fellows, "DO NOT FALTER!"

Anjes and Yorn are set upon, and Herjas is among three of Janderas' men when he is seized by the leg and pulled away at a speed no earthly man can follow. In vain clutching at shrubs and roots (shouting at the critter that he will slay it), he breaks his arm upon hitting against a rock; and when the beast draws to a halt and lets go of his leg, turning to him with gaping jaws, its growls penetrate his ears and its fangs soon his neck.

Until the beasts cease their hunt, few remain of the once large group. The soil beneath Artias' feet is drenched with blood, and Gordes' sword is bend out of shape and Hentario's broken, and Janderas' spear is gone alongside of his men. A mere moment ago they were thirteen men, now only four are left, and they grief and mourn for the dead and cry out their pain.

"I told their wives I will watch them," Janderas utters almost silently. "I told them I will, I said I will, promised I will. Lies, it were all lies that I told their wives."

Artias, though as much in pain as the others, draws a breath and tells everyone that they must leave the site of the fight before other creatures will come.

"It was mere luck," Janderas utters, dropping to his knees. "It was mere luck that we found them. Is it that they desired vengeance for the death of —"

"We must get away!" demands Artias. "We have no time to grief!"

"We helped them fight off creatures, the same creatures that came upon us now, Artias. HEED

MY WORDS, THE BEASTS, THEY SOUGHT TO AVENGE THEIR OWN; AND NOW, NOW WE MUST AVENGE THE FALLEN." His tears run dry and he rises, declaring that he bring down each and every beast he may find.

"No, Janderas," says Artias. "Who travels through the forest must be aware of an attack, and I tell you, the claws of the forest hunt to feed and not to avenge—"

"YOU HEARD THEIR SCREAMS, SO DO NOT TELL ME ANYTHING! I HEARD MY FELLOWS CALLING MY NAME, BEGGING ME TO HELP THEM—I COULD NOT!"

"Acting foolishly will not bring them back."

"That being is the only reason we came here, but now I am to return alone, telling every wife hoping to see her man again that my words have been a lie."

"He is broken," says Hentario. "We lost our friends, people we have known for so long that, that … . Brothers they were. Yes. But they have been taken. Slain. I must. No, I say, their passing, as much as it makes my heart cry, it will not make me yield. This I owe them. Yes, we all do."

"Aye," agrees Gordes, "we owe them this; and I say, horsemen, tell of your companions' bravery, unless you wish to let their names be forgotten! I say, our brothers shall never be forgotten; I shall never let their names be forgotten!"

With brooding eyes Janderas stares at the ground, recalling the day as he had left the norther plain with his companions.

"What now?" he asks himself. "What shall I do now? I must return. Yes, I must return now."

"Janderas," says Artias, trying to speak calmly. "We must get away from the site of the fight first, and then, then we shall decide what to do next."

"Their wives must know, Artias. They must be told of the horror I led their husbands into."

"You have no fault."

"I do, for I did command them, and I did lead them … I have led them — I do no more now."

"Go then," shouts Gordes. "Every day we shared with our brothers brought light into our lives, and there was joy and love. In fellowship we stood, to death we had — I say, honor the death or I shall, oh, I shall come at you and … ."

"You are gone in thought, horsemen," says Hentario. "You are nothing alike the man you seemed to be — you are broken."

Janderas looks at the hunter as he tells him that before he leaves, he must make sure that he is treated fairly in Odas. "I owe you this, unless you —"

"Oh, you owe him more than that," utters Gordes. "You have brought us here, so you better be careful what you say, or I will hurt you, so very severely I will beat you!"

"Leave him be," demands Artias; "there was no way he could have known what would happen!"

With gnashing teeth Hentario scowls at Janderas, saying, "You better thank him. Thank him with all your heart, horsemen, for he is saving your life just now."

"Kill me, if so you desire — but I say to you, for the love of my wife, I shall not let you have my life just so!"

"What are we doing?" Gordes utters, moving back a pace. "Hentario, we shall not come off our way again. I say, listen to me, evil, wipe it off your heart. He has no fault. He is not to blame. But we will be if we come off our way."

On the edge of the fall to evil, they shall not lose their footing again. On the path they have chosen to walk with Artias, there shall be no shame; and there shall be no wrong as that which had made them welcome violence. They know, despite their pain, that Janderas has no fault, for he did not know what prowls about; and they, under Artias watchful eye, approach him and ask him for forgiveness, for almost they would have fallen.

"I do not blame you," says Janderas; "I have only myself to blame. Nobody bu—"

"Listen to me, my fellows," Artias strikes in, "we head for Odas now, for I shall return; but, above all, we must part from here!"

In admiration for his wife's brother, Janderas kneels down before him.

"You are righteous, Artias. Can you forgive me my behavior? I did speak in favor of the people of Odas. Yes, I did. Forgive me."

"It is forgotten, Janderas, and you need not kneel before me—let us move now. Quick!"

Throughout the following days, while these four hearty men travel to Odas, rarely speaking of the fight than telling stories of their dead fellows; Janderas is so quiet that Artias fears for his well-being, and the longer he remains in silence, the greater Artias' worries become.

Shortly before dusk, Artias and his fellows prepare for the night. Gordes collects tinder and fiercely strikes two pieces of quartz together 'til the first few sparks set the tinder alight. His fellows gather twigs and branches, and with all the wood they find, the flames are fed and made to grow larger and larger, and they thereupon set up traps together with Artias and asks Hentario to be the first to stand guard.

As the night comes, they anxiously await dawn, trying to distract their fears by telling stories, and it is then when Artias asks Janderas what being he spoke of.

"What do you mean?" Janderas wonders.

"You said you came here because of a being?"

"Yes, yes, I remember, but it matters no more now."

"You mind telling me of it?"

"There is nothing to tell, Artias: I know neither where it comes from nor what it is."

"So what made you think you'll find it here?"

"The last time I saw it, it was heading towards this forest. It is unlike anything I have ever seen in my life. Neither man nor creature, neither man nor creature."

It dawns on Artias just what Janderas hoped to find, and he tells him this, saying then that it has spoken to him many days ago.

"True," says Hentario, "it did speak to you — so we have witnessed. I say, a creature bearing a blade, how very odd is that."

"Yes" — Janderas looks at his fellows — "it carries a blade and wears clothes, but it is no man, and neither is it a creature."

"It is divine." Artias speaks in awe. "It must be what created all that is around us."

"I wouldn't say that." Hentario stretches his back and checks his sword before he looks around the forest quickly. "It is simply something we didn't know exists."

Truth be told, it is no god and it is not divine but something that has lived in Arjovan long before the coming of Man, and it is not the only one of its kind: they are legions.

"It spoke to me," says Artias. "It must have understood what it said, for it forgave me, I know."

The Bane of Assistance
The condemned man: Forced to take the blame upon himself, damned to walk the Earth and know he will be blamed to end of his days through no fault of his own, evokes his hate and hardens his sorrow.

Odas appears ahead of them after five days of walking through a realm where the until yet most imposing sights lie. Discomfort arouses in Artias upon seeing the people who signed the letter, in which he was blamed for what had happened in this village. He must halt before falling into their sight and take a breath, in silence hoping that they will be just to him and perhaps even forgive him for killing Beras, Tindras, and Gilgaron.

Seeing just how hard it is for the hunter to approach these very people, Janderas lays a hand on Artias' shoulder, saying, "You will not be treated unfairly — I will make sure of that."

"Yes," says Hentario, "so will I."

"We all will," Gordes assures Artias. "We all stand with you, my friend."

By the moment Artias appears treading along the path through Odas, the few people who survived their aimless travel through the creatures' realm step out of their homes and glare a him, openly declaring that he is not welcome here.

"Begone," they say. "You have brought only misery. We should kill you for your ignorance. Showing yourself here, how much more suffer must we bear!"

"Silence," Janderas cries at every soul scowling at the hunter. "He is hear to put things right, and I will not allow any of you to — "

More and more people come around, insisting that Artias take his leaving. Tarion stands amid these men and women and calls out to everyone that Artias is here to claim yet more lives, saying too, "As if we had not suffered enough."

"He brought the beast," shouts Arianna, swiftly walking to the group. "I buried my son and witness the killing of a friend only because he could not keep his desires at bay."

"I DO NOT DESIRE KILLING." Artias breaths heavily, feels as if thousands of stones were put upon his shoulders and thousands of needles driven into his heart. "I WAS HERE TO HELP YOU!"

Many of the men, who came to see the one they say had caused only death and suffer, hurry to their houses to get knives and sticks; and as they return, they show their weapons to Artias, gesturing with these that he shall leave. "We will stab and batter you to death if you do not," say they.

At once Gordes raises his crooked sword, shouting at them, "I say to you, try to do so and I shall behead each one of you!"

"You let him have his say," commands Janderas. But, even though all of these people owe their lives to him, they keep on blaming the hunter, saying (that) "Artias brought the beast", and then accuse Janderas of joined the hunter's villainous plans to grow his own wealth.

"You deceived us like Artias had," they say, and Arianna then continues: "You let us think that you mean well whereas you merely took us back here to have the hunter find us."

"Watch your mouth, woman," cries the horseman. "I do no evil!"

"You help Artias, and Artias had summoned the beast—"

"I did not summon any beast, Arianna!"

"Oh, you, you just wish to see us suffer!"

"Why would you say something like that?" Slowly Artias approaches her, asking again why, "Why would you say something like that?"

To see how she looks at him fills him with sadness, and pain strikes his heart and suffer conquers his mind, and on the verge of tears he says: "As I saw you on the ground, holding your boy, my only desire was to give you comfort, to help you find peace. I would have given my life for that of your boy." He tears his clothes apart, laying bare his chest. "Stab me down, thrust your knife into my hear if that will make you feel better, but it will never change the way I feel for you, for every one of you!"

"Why, why would you come here?" she asks. "Why? Why do you not simply turn around and leave?"

"Because I am here to put things right. I found the letter, and I saw your name upon it, your name and that of others; and I asked myself how could it be that you let the words of one man so deep into your thoughts that you wish I were dead."

"Yes," says Gordes, "how could you?" and he looks at the people, asking them the same again and then saying to them: "Shame on you, upon every last one of you, for regarding this honorable man as wicked whereas the one you thought to be righteous was the wicked."

"But... his words made so much sense. Beras, he said you—"

"I see." Artias closes his eyes for a moment, trying to imagine himself sitting beneath a tree far away from here. "You made your decision, believed him all that he had told you, even though Ardega—"

"Do not mention his name," the people cry, but Artias does not heed their words and raises his voice, shouting, "ARDEGAN DID NOT LISTEN TO ME. HE SIMPLY RAN OUT INTO THE DARKNESS."

"How shall we tell whether or not you speak the truth?" asks Arianna.

"Forget them, Artias," advises Gordes. "They are sheep needing a shepherd, and if that be a foul one!"

"The words of one man caused me to be banished from a village; the words of one man caused me to be seen as an evildoer; the words of one man made me kill in rage. The words of one person, one soul, one being like me had turned you all against me; and now I ask you, I ask you why, why did you betray me, knowing very well that no earthly men can summon beast?"

"Beras merely said out loud what everyone was thinking, Artias!"

"Is that so, or did he simply give you an answer to a question you could not answer yourself?"

"I do not understand what you want from me."

"I was told that everyone turns to you when in trouble. You are like an Elder to these people, which is why I speak to you, and it is why I ask myself how come you let Beras decide what is right and wrong rather than doing so yourself. I ask myself why, why you, Arianna, as the one who people turn to, let him decide for you. Can you tell me why, Arianna?"

"He tries to manipulate you," says Tarion. "Do not fall for—"

"Be still now!" Hentario yells at him. "You have caused enough already with your lack of thought."

Looking only at Artias, Arianna says that she loved Ardegan, and when he died, there had to be someone to blame, because there always is someone to blame. The only way to make the pain go away was to turn it into anger, anger that focused on Artias. Beras did not hate him but searched for a face to blame, just like everyone else did.

"I cannot change the past," she tells him. "And even if I know you have no fault, I cannot stop hating you. I know it is wrong, but I need someone to blame."

Outraged, Gordes kicks the dirt beneath his feet. "Blame the beast then or better even—"

"No," Artias interrupts harshly. "The beast was merely searching for fare. It cannot and shall not be blamed," and he, though feeling as if there is something Arianna does not dare to say, continues in a way he never spoke before: "The only one to blame is you, Arianna, you and the lots of you." Wordlessly he turns around and tells his fellows to follow him. "I do not want to spend but a moment longer in this place."

Before he leaves Odas, he looks back one last time, telling everyone: "There will come the day when your blindness and ignorance will be your nemesis, but then I will not be here to give you a face to blame. I wonder, who might be blamed then. Perhaps you, Tarion, or maybe it will be you, Arianna. It might as well be any one of you"; and then he takes his leaving, wishing to never return.

The farer away Odas lies the better he feels. He travels with friends, with people who do him no wrong. They are indeed good-hearted fellows, and it fills him with pleasure to call them his companions, and he shows his gratitude by claiming them righteous in heart and honorable in their way.

"You do good to forget Odas," says Janderas. "Under the Sun, there all life is equal. Why do you not come with me back to your kin."

"I cannot, for I must continue my path. The divine being, it made me understand the importance of my undertaking — I will not be stopped."

"Wherever your way will take you," Gordes says, "you will never be traveling alone. That is, unless I die; but even if so, you still have Hentario."

"And what about you?" Gordes then asks Janderas. "Are you thinking about going home or is it that you wish to travel on with us?"

"No, I must return home. If it would not be for my beloved wife, I would struggle to, though."

"Perhaps I should join you," says Artias. "I know my kin and that you will not be blamed for what happened; but, after all, I would have never expected that the people of Odas hate me simply because they need a face to blame."

"It is not blame I am worried about, Artias, it is the knowing that my arrival will arouse pain. When they see me coming alone, they will know something happened. Be that as it may, you have your way and I have mine — do not worry about me."

"I do, though."

"Yes, I can see that."

"What about the horses?" asks Hentario. "Fine animals they were."

"When I am back, I shall gather a party and set about finding them. Perhaps I am lucky and cross ways with them on my way back to the northern plain — who's to say."

Janderas strikes the foliage before him to see what lies ahead, visibly glad that there shows a glade.

"Veran," he mumbles, seeing the village appearing in the distance. "How about we drink together in Veran before parting?"

Artias shakes his head.

"No," says he. "We been banished from there."

"Banished?"

"Yes."

"So Veran is the village you spoke about back in Odas?"

"Yes."

"Thanks to your man we are not welcome there," says Hentario. "I must say, though, the Elder is an idiot."

"I can speak to the Elder. Despite Perjn's treachery, I sent him there—"

"No," Artias interrupts. "Who banishes someone knowing very well that it is wrong is nobody I wish to see or speak to again."

"Are you sure?"

"I am."

"Well, then I will tell my lovely wife that I saw and traveled with her brother—she'll be delighted."

"There will come the day when I will come to the northern plain. I hope you will be there then."

"Do take care of yourself on your travels, Artias. Of course, I wish all of you only the best."

Janderas utters a last farewell, saying, "I hope to arm you afore winter," and thereon departs for the northern plain. Thenceforth Artias and his companions embark upon a journey to the east, where the hugest of trees ever to grow on earth shade vast areas of leaf. In this seemingly evergreen land, he wishes to continue his undertaking; however, for all his achievements, every pace casts a gloom of doubt upon him, for the events in Odas and Veran prey on his mind, and he asks himself whether he is fated to die by the hands of whomever he may seek to aid in the days to come. Even if he believes that the divine being commanded that he keep going his way, he wonders if he should simply forget about his undertaking and head for Delmar.

Gordes can see that something is troubling his friend, though he does not say a word; he himself often broods over his life and rather be alone with his thoughts than having to share his pains.

Whilst walking across the glade, journeying east, they see wild horses grazing and other creatures digging holes in search of worms or insects; and they watch birds flying through the sky high above them and begin to wonder how it may be to have wings.

Though they have to proceed through the forest at the glade's edge and traverse a beautiful field with ever so many flowers, they do not struggle to range, however far. Each one of them is enduring, considering anything below ten miles to be but a stroll.

They move along the foot of the mountain towards *the eastern forest**, seeing its gigantic trees from afar. Henceforth the days of yore, these trees have grown to astounding height, the oldest of which are up to 330 feet (100 meters) in height.

Artias and his companions feel honored to stand among these colossal plants at the end of their journey to this ground, and their amazement should never cease.

"These trees, they are amazing," says Gordes, feeling as if he be dreaming. "I feel so small, my fellows, so very little."

"I cannot imagine that anyone would ever settle here," says Hentario to Artias, looking upon this forest as the earliest of all and never to be inhabited by Man.

In sight of the wilderness they wander, the idea to come here appears to be a mistake more and more; this forest seems to have neither beginning nor end.

"Perhaps we should not be here," comments Artias.

"Yes," says Gordes, and Hentario agrees too.

They feel the embrace of a mysterious aura mantling them in a warm sensation; and they stand wreathed in lush foliage and hear the trees humming, anon discovering that also the loving 'brace they feel comes from these colossal plants, though more and more they begin to think of themselves as intruders. This forest is no place for them to be, no place to wander or cross; and they feel and urge, an overwhelming desire to take their leaving; and at night, when many green lights float about the bottoms of the trees, this feeling strengthens.

"Anhe tendrium," says Artias, repeating these words many times.

"What does that mean?" asks Gordes, and Artias says, "Divine tree."

All three men spend the entire night heeding the trees' songs 'til day's first light lets them see just how lucky they were to have survived the night, although it does not take much more to stay alive than a little understanding of the realm not part of Man's own.

"I cannot do this anymore," Artias says, seeing rays of sunlight shining through the treetops down upon a ground abundant in plant life; and there show roots with blankets of moss covering them whole, and he sees the trees' many lights fading at the brightness of *Sun's grace**.

"I say, my fellows, see this realm. The more I make known how important a stockade is to live in areas like this one, the more villages will be raised, and the more there are, the more the creatures' realm will be forgotten. How long until such places will be known only by tales and stories of old."

"I remember that you said you will not be stopped," says Gordes.

"Now I can see what I was told. Yes. The divine one made me go on until I see with my own eyes what I have been causing. Now that I do, I can happily withdraw from my undertaking."

"And head for the northern plain?"

"Yes, I wish to return to my roots; and I ask you, my friends, join me. I say, let us settle down."

"We have nothing better to do," they say.

Together they leave the forest and make their way to the northern plain.

Shoulder to shoulder
Ashamed, afraid to make his kin grief at the sight of his lone return, he struggled at his every pace, but resolute and unwavering he went on his way.

Delmar is the largest village in Arjovan to date, raised in the northern plain, not far from the *eastern mountain**; and there reside Artias' kinsfolk among others who had joined their cause like Janderas did when he was but a lonesome sword striving for justice in a land that knows no law.

Seeing Delmar's stockade ahead, standing in the even ground of this vast plain, he looks back on the day of his leaving. With six hale men, all of whom had faith in him and his leadership, he left in search of the being Artias regards as divine. Back then, he would have never though that he will be the only one to return.

Beholding the plain, observing a herd of wild horses roaming the land, he dwells upon the fine animals he had lost and comes to see, before his inner eye, the beast that seized his fellow and all the claws that followed its assail. To think of seeing the wives of all the men who have been slain evokes discomfort, and he feels shame and guilt bearing down upon him. Trying to repel his pain and fend off his own blame to hold on his way, he stares at the village, wishing he would have to cover many miles more before seeing it in the distance.

But there! A mounted group leaves Delmar and comes his way.

More and more ashamed of himself, he tries to figure out what he may say to them; for these horsemen, each one of them, he knows.

'Forgive me,' he may say; yet when they bring their horses to a halt in front of him, he remains in silence.

Ginhal, a slender man with bristles on his chin and short hair, leaps down his horse, asking Janderas what came upon him.

"Beasts, my friend, beasts."

At a glance it is clear to everyone that all the warriors Janderas left with are gone. It is not that he is alone that makes this known, but the fact that he is without horse. In silence Ginhal lays both of his hands on Janderas cheeks, gently forcing him to look in his eyes.

"What beasts killed our friends?"

"The claws of the forest did."

Ginhal's companions, men with strong arms and women with fair eyes, silently mourn for the passing of their fellows and tell Janderas that he must not be ashamed of himself.

"We know you and do not blame you," they say.

"What shall I tell their wives? That I failed to lead them safely?"

Declaring that every undertaking bears a risk, Ginhal lets go of his friend and mounts his horse.

"We are up to take down a bandit tribe in the west. Your skills are needed, Janderas—if you wish to join us."

"It might be wiser to set about finding our horses—"

"We have been up to this for quite some time now, my friend. We cannot let weeks of careful planing be for nothing. Join us—if you wish to, that is."

To Grief, Avenge, and Come together
His fears turned to anger and anger into hate, and his hate he let loose and set upon his tormentors — his savageness was beyond all that had been witnessed before.

More than several days of travail it takes Artias and his two companions to reach a path on *the mountain in the west** from where they can move through deep snow towards the northern plain. Gordes is not used to the cold they are engulfed by and complains about their lack of preparation. There are few caves that can be used as shelter, but they are not even near the summit, so any cave they come across might be inhabited by bandits. Many times Artias tells his two companions to watch out for bandits, but at the end of the third day of their march on the mountain, his caution seems pointless, because Gordes cannot bear the cold any longer and separates from the group in sight of a cave. He dashes towards it, slipping on ice and snow in his rush and falls down a rock face.

Artias and Hentario forthwith hurry to his assistance, hoping that he merely feel several feet.

"GORDES!" they call down, anxiously awaiting an answer.

"I fell into the snow," they hear him yelling.

"Are you hurt?" asks Artias.

"I do not think so... yet."

"Stay where you are. We are coming down to you somehow."

Hentario looks around for a place to descend. The mountain towers endlessly high next to him, leaving him and Artias on a small path bounded by the falling face of the rock on one side and the vastly rising wall on the other.

"Maybe the cave can take us down," says he, seeing no other way to get to their friend, besides of risking a jump in hopes that the snow will catch their fall, too.

Nodding Artias cries down to Gordes whether he sees a cave, but there comes no answer this time.

"Gordes," he shouts, "answer me!"

"What's going on," Hentario utters anxiously, fearing for his friend. "What if he is hurt?" he thinks and seizes Artias by the arm, hollering, "Who knows what critters live upon mountains. He could be too hurt to fight! We must get down to him. Now!"

Artias is as worried as his friend and agrees at once, carefully treading to the cave until he sees Hentario falling unconscious next to him. He wants to check on his friend yet a hit on his head prevents this and lets him share his fellow's sate.

He awakes shortly after in the grasp of men whose wicket glint in their eyes send shivers down his spine. Thrown down into a hole barely higher than he himself but as broad as a house, he is reunited with Hentario, who lies motionless on the floor. He looks up at the men, seeing their with hide covered bodies and the swords they hold at him from above. The amount of leather strings they wear on their wrists stand for their numbers and let him know how outnumbered he is.

"I did not hit you very hard," says one of them. "Seems you're not as tough as your fellow—"

"Bandits are you, yes? Wicked tribes of yours!"

"Who says we are bandits?"

"I do recognize you foul beings. Even in the cold you manage to stink beyond anything!"

"You have a pretty big mouth. You wishing to join your fellow?"

To hear this makes Artias' skin crawl, and he bends down to Hentario, assuming the worst. Shouting at his fellow to wake up again and again, he soon realizes that he won't anymore.

"WHAT HAVE YOU DONE TO HIM!" he cries at them.

"You can easily slip in these caves. Snow turns to ice and on ice you can slip and fall and bag your head quite easily."

Hentario did not slip: he was thrown into the hole and fell on the back of his head, fracturing his skull. He died shortly after.

"You will pay for this with your lives!" vows Artias, searching for a rock to throw at them. "I WILL BREAK YOUR NECKS FOR THIS!"

"The only one who'll lie dying on the ground will be you — I toy with the idea of throwing you down the steepest part of this cave!"

"Oh, you will be coming with me. I vow that you will!"

The man takes up a rock and flings it at the hunter.

"I will have your mouth sewn close anytime soon now!"

"However many you might be, I will slay you, and I will do so with a smile on my face! Down into your heart my blade will be driven with joy and pleasure at the thought of your death!"

"You want to smile like your friend when we found him? Or no, wait, he wasn't so glad as he fell."

"What?"

"Your friend, your other friend, his mouth was as big as his strengths; but, unfortunate for him, he did not grow wings."

"Speak with sense, you—"

"YOU CAN FIND HIM SPLATTERED SOMEWHERE AT THE BOTTOM OF THE MOUNTAIN!"

Artias says nothing, can't find a word to say. Everything just changed in one instant.

"Why so quiet now? Did you just realize the trouble you are in? Your friends are dead, and you'll be joining them quite soon, and then I will be the one smiling, with pleasure blowing my knife into you."

As the men leave, telling one of theirs to watch the prisoner, Artias feels rage storming so strongly within him that he almost can't keep himself from bursting out and try with all his might to kill as many bandits as he can. To get out of the hole unseen is impossible, though; the man watching him is not once looking anywhere else than at him.

"Why are you always looking at me?" asks he.

"I ca' see you planin' somethin'—I'll not allow it!"

"Then come down to me, come down to me and keep me from it."

Artias gets no answer, and the man keeps on staring at him, smiling at the though of his fate. Then a pebble is thrown at the man; and though he blames the throw on one of his own, saying, "I whack your face should you do that again," he comes to see the men behind him, forthwith falling down into the hole, right before Artias' feet.

"And arrow?" Artias utters, seeing it sticking in the fiend's forehead. "Who shot this arrow?"

He tries to espy who's up there lurking around, in a whisper saying, "Who's creeping there?"

To then see his kin emerging from the shadows alongside of Janderas fills him with utter astonishment.

Looking as confused as Artias, Janderas steps forth, asking him what on earth he is doing here.

Quickly Artias climbs out of the hole, being given a hand to hold as he gets out. He does not look at his kin, cares not to see how confused they are to meet him here.

"What brought you here?" Janderas would like to know, but all that the hunter says is that he shall hand him a sword "right now".

"Give me a blade to cleave their skulls!" Artias speaks in rage, thirsting for blood and justice. "An eye for an eye and a tooth for a tooth—they will pay!"

"Pay for what?" asks Ginhal. "What is going on, Artias?"

"Give me your sword, Janderas! Their blood, I will make it leave their bodies and drench the rock!"

Blinded by rage, Artias is about to dash deeper into the cave, unarmed, alone, and most likely to be outnumbered by his foes. Heedless of the strengths of the fleeing, he is willing to risk everything to claim their lives. His drive to avenge his friends is stronger than any other feeling, giving rise to a most reckless pursuit of his foes.

"I WILL KILL THEM ALL," he shouts.

Janderas forthwith grabs him by the arm before he can take a step and tells him—and this Artias has already predicted by the moment he grew aware of the attack—, "The only bandits still left are those who fled deeper into the cave."

"You cannot charge headlong down there," says Ginhal, "unless you know the way, but even so—"

"I CARE NOT," Artias cries, suddenly grabbing Janderas by the belt and unsheathing his friend's blade, and thereupon he pushes him away and runs deeper into the cave, crying out at everyone there, "I WILL BEHEAD YOU!"

The cave used to provide shelter for a large group of marauders, robbers, and slayers. Since the attack, however, many of them have fallen. Apart from those who are not here, there are but a few who could escape the sudden assail, and these few men—all of whom never showed their victims mercy, for they deemed them no other than prey—have been seeking a way out to alert their own of the attack ever since.

They hear Artias' cry and the dozens of steps following their pursuer and run quicker and quicker, eager to survive to fight another day.

"Tendjan will be told of this!" cry they. "And he will come and eat you alive."

The cave has many tunnels that lead in a circle, tunnels they never dared to walk through before in fear of whatever beings they might find there, and eventually they end up behind Artias with the rest of their foes drawing nearer from the rear. They do not think about retracing their steps and decide to set upon the man ahead: to have slain at least one of their foes will cloak the shame of running. Artias is in front of them, many steps apart from his kin: it should be easy to stab him in the back whilst fleeing from the others.

But the heavy tread of their boots alerts Artias of their approach; and he, almost lanced by a knife on turning to face them, strikes at the man in the lead, thrusting him into the arms of the others. Stepping back a pace, he grimly stares at the wicked, speaking in rage as he pledges, "I will have your blood on this sword!"

None of the men are daunted by his threat.

"Away with you," say they, coming at him with knives and swords.

Spearing the belly of the man in the fore, Artias shoves the blade through stomach and liver; and he thereupon beheads the villain nearest to him and boots the body at the others, repelling them.

Striving for justice, he charges at whomever left with raised sword, fending off their attacks, cleaving their skulls, piercing their necks, driving the sword through organs and flesh.

Artias' kin never saw him fight and stand frozen in their tracks on arriving at the site. To witness the savageness of his attacks lets them shudder.

"CALM DOWN," they cry at him as the last bandit has fallen and Artias keeps stabbing the body, crying, "DIE, DIE, DIE, DIE!"

Janderas must lunge at Artias (swiftly evading his friend's blind strike) to awaken him.

Wordlessly Artias drops the blade and treads past his kin, caring little about seeing them again. All he can think about now are his dead friends. Those who had shown such loyalty and bravery took on eternal rest. He crushes down, gulping back his tears, tightening his muscles—the pain is overwhelming.

"Artias," Janderas says, announcing his coming. "Come, let us go home"—he lays his hands upon his friend's shoulder—"let us go home and there will be peace in your heart at the end."

Among your Kin
He tried to help as best as he could, did his utmost to lend aid in times of disarray, only to then see that where hate and recklessness do not exist, unjust does not either.

Delmar possesses a stockade and many fine houses near and far from the yard. Unlike elsewhere, watchtowers flank the gate and guards are found walking around with hounds. The main path, bounded primarily by bowyers, blacksmiths and emporiums on one side and trading posts on the other, is a blessing to anyone searching for gear or other. Until now, Delmar is the only place resembling fortification and development of future villages and cities—and these will come to be great.

Together with Janderas, Artias enters the village in the fore of the group. Although he used to live here, thus knowing were what lies, much has changed since he left for his undertaking; nevertheless, he sees neither the freshly built stable near the gate nor any of the recently raised houses, and he cares little about the joy he arouses in his kindred for being here. Truly, he is greeted kindly and warmly, receiving many words of affection, yet he cares not and heads alone along the main path in his grief.

"He has been like this the whole time," say Ginhal to Janderas, observing Artias walking with head bowed: he has never seen him like this at any day before the incident on the mountain. "I am worried."

"So am I."

"He seems to be somewhere else, far gone somehow."

"In pain, he is in pain."

Artias is in great pain; he lost loyal friends, friends whose passing has been crushing his heart to this day; and he walks along the path, passing by many houses while mourning silently.

CLOSE BY: Tanara, whose love for every being other than the wicked is known to everyone in Delmar, enjoys the company of Hervjol and Hjos, although the matter they are discussing is grave. They do not know that Janderas had joined Ginhal and the others; and as they are oblivious to their kin's return, they continue to assume that something must have happened to Janderas.

Tanara worries for her spouse, fears for his life even; and also the wives of every man who went with Janderas are in worry, though whereas they discover the truth at his return, Tanara does not.

Sitting at a table with the others, she says she would like to leave in search of her husband, for he should have returned many days ago.

"But whether he is still looking for that being you do not know," says Hjos. "Perhaps he is yet on his way back or—"

"Or dead already!"

"No, no," Hervjol utters. "A strong man he is, not easily frightened or slain. I am sure he is—"

Hervjol hushes as he hears the sound of ever so loud voices praising Ginhal and his brave fellows.

"Have they returned?" he wonders, approaching a window facing the main path.

"There!" says he. "Come and look, Tanara, there is your spouse."

And then he sees Artias walking by his house and heads outside at once.

"Artias," he calls, coming around the hunter with Hjos. "Artias, how long has it been since we have last seen each other."

But Artias is awkwardly silent, and Janderas says that bad things have happened to him and to those he had been with.

"Have beasts attacked you?" asks a woman. "Have you lost your beloved, too?" And she treads forth, embracing Artias and saying that he must not speak if he does not wish to, and she says, "Why, oh, why have our husbands been taken from us!" And she sheds tears and clenches her hands around his as if he were her pillar of strengths.

"You know the wild better than anyone, better than Werhanjo or the others; so tell me, oh, I beg of you, tell me why have our husbands been taken from us?"

Janderas explains every wife of every man he had with him that their beloveds fought bravely against beasts.

"With raised sword they fought to the end," says he, and he looks at his wife, seeing her loving gaze, and lays his arm around her, in a whisper saying in her ear, "I love you."

The woman cannot let off Artias, for he lost loved ones, too. Every wife draws to him and embraces him and cries with him, although he sheds no tear.

"But say, what happened?" asks Tanara, knowing that he must have lost someone whom he treasured beyond words.

"What happened," Artias utters fiercely, "is foulness. A bandit tribe slew my companions. I could not help them nor could I fight for them. I awoke and they were dead."

"We lost our husbands," say the widows. "We hav—"

"And I grief for them, too; and I share your pain. But it is not the same. Beasts, creatures, they hunt and kill to survive, whereas the foul do not. No. There are no natural reasons for their doings, only spite. I say, let me join you, let me join you in your fight?"

Hervjol, the first Elder of Arjovan, has seen many things in his life he would like to forget and can see very clearly just how much Artias grieves for his friends.

"We are sorry for your loss and share your pain, but must I tell you, Artias, I must tell you what I have told you once before: Do not seek vengeance; fight for the right reasons."

"Why is it that critters can live without committing immoral acts. I tell you, Hervjol, sin is what separates us from them. It is what makes Man Man, and it disgust me down to my core! My innermost belief in virtue—shattered!"

Strain and urge

There he awoke unharmed lying in the snow. Blessed he seemed to be, for not a scratch he had from the fall. The long way back to his fellows should be strenuous, though; and he would not know whether he ... be alive long enough to find them.

For more than six days Gordes has been traveling along the foot of the mountain, seeking a way up, back to the cave he dashed for so boldly.

Worrying for his fellows, he holds on his way, stopping only when he must to eat or grant his aching back a break. Though he was thrown down yet another cliff by brigands, all of whom were part of the bandit tribe dwelling in the cave, a rock jutting out from the cliff saved his life, reducing his fall to 30 feet (9 meters). Even so, he was lucky: if not for the snow covering the rock's surface, death would have been certain. But for all his luck, from this rock he could not climb back up; the cliff rises too steeply for a climb, holding too much ice upon its surface. Underneath it, though, the mountain slopes down to even ground, whence he could reach its foot. And days of travail awaited him thereupon: days of hunting and seeking ponds while through all searching for a way to ascent this soaring mass of earth again, for he must hurry to his fellows' aid . . . .

Seeing a steep fall beside him after traveling from the mountain's foot into height, he believes to be where he had lost his footing and gazes down, thinking of the incident that followed his mindless rush towards the sheltering cave. When he lay in the snow after the fall, those brigands emerged around him, forcing him into silence;

and they said to him, "Do you know how good one can hear a shout up here. Think of your companions, oh, what might befall them, you hearty man—you should have held your tongue."

Determined to die to ward his fellows, Gordes raged and fought—but in vain.

"I will slay them," he utters fiercely, with eyes set to descry the cave if ever it should arise, where he then may find his fellows alive and well.

Unfortunately, Gordes comes to realize that he has no idea where exactly he is; that which pointed him the way here to this spot upon vast rock were distinctive features of the rocky walls rising to his right, features that were not as distinctive as he thought—frankly, he went the wrong way, sadly.

And now he feels weak and struggles to walk and breathe. He is too high, not used to such heights, but knows neither how far he came off his way nor how severely such a climb can affect his body. He nevertheless retraces his steps, descending.

Having eaten all his supplies and struggling with the pain in his back, he decides to head for the northern plain to find Janderas. Certainly he will be able to help him find his fellows, and if that be (only) just in time.

The closer he comes to the foot of the mountain, the weaker he feels, up until he falls, face fore, into the snow.

"I cannot," stutters he, "no more." His strengths is fading, his endurance dwindling, he toils to rise; yet he manages—only just.

And with all the vitality he has left to muster for a finally drain, he moves on towards the tree line; but when the timberline lies behind him, he is on the verge of death, edging to eternal rest, and due to this unable to see that he is, in truth, approaching the southern forest.

He shakes, but he keeps going; his jaws feel numb, but he keeps going; he feels dizzy but keeps going pace by pace. And he indeed reaches the ground of the forest, a remarkable achievement, even though it would not have been possible if his body weren't so enduring: miles over miles he used to travel with his fellows on foot, from one place to the other. Striding and marching, fighting and hunting, all done on his own two legs and not once from upon a horse.

However great his physical endurance may be, his body has suffered too much already: he will not be able to stand upright much longer. Then, all at once growing aware of the ground he wanders, he is overcome with distress, crushed at the knowing that he has met with disaster. He took upon himself great pains to save his fellows, was unwavering, unrelentingly in pursuit of his aim, and yet destined to founder.

In the distance he sees roaming horses and finds comfort in the thought that he is not alone and sits down somewhere within the creatures' realm, knowing that consciousness is just about to bid farewell. Then people are heard talking and horses snorting, and a known voice says with pleasure and joy, "I am glad no harm came unto them. Let us hitch them to your saddle."

The voice of his fellow lets Gordes rise and dash through the greenery, calling as best as he can, "ARTIAS!"

His shouting is not in vain. Artias hears his friend's calling and looks around hastily from upon a mare, seeing nothing but the trees and the very horses that had run off shortly before he and his stouthearted companions were assailed by the claws of the forest. Janderas is with him and recognizes the voice of the man in the woods and begins to call his name, shouting "Gordes" louder than ever; and their friend emerges from the surrounding foliage, then and there dropping to his knees.

They ride to him with seven horses in tow, dismount at once, and gawk at whom they thought was dead as if seeing a ghost.

"Gordes," says Artias, seeing his friend losing consciousness; and "Do not part, you hear!" he says upon seeing him falling unconscious.

"Help me lay him across my horse," he tells Janderas. "Veran is not far. We take him there!"

At once helping Artias hoist a man who's much heavier than thought onto the mare, Janderas states that Gordes needs to be attended to urgently. "He is very weak."

"I know," Artias utters in worry. "I know, I know — we must be quick now!"

The sky darkens as they ride to Veran at the pace of a gallop. That Artias was banished from that village alongside of his companions would not stop him from seeking help there; Gordes needs a healer: he needs help, or he will die.

Before Veran lies within sight Janderas says that he will tell each and every soul who may dare to try and send them away of the man Gordes killed as sent by him. "The Elder shall heed my words and help our friend, or he will be brought to—"

"No," Artias interrupts. "Not a drop of blood will be spilled today. If he doesn't help us, I will force him to, but slay him in rage, that I won't."

Veran is brightened by the torches along its path, illuminating the night; thus they are exposed to every guard near and far on arriving and are not long after approached by them.

"Stay back!" Janderas shouts at them. "This man needs help, or he will die!"

One of the guards, by far the most formidable man Artias has ever seen in his life, reminds him of the banishment and declares that they shall treat him like a villain for his foolish return, and perhaps even claim these horses of theirs.

"THEN THERE WILL BE BLOOD," Janderas cries, leaping down from his horse. He shouts at Artias to seek the Elder and draws his blade.

"I will hold them back," he tells him, and at the guards he glares as he raves, "EACH ONE OF YOU I WILL HOLD BACK," and he cries at them, "COME NOW, AND DEATH WILL BE QUICK!"

His shouting draws the people outside. They come with gaping mouths out of their homes, witnessing how greatly the guards they thought to be steadfast endeavor to keep authority. In fear of the stranger's wrath, who keeps yelling at the guards that they will die a savage death should they dare and come near, people tell their children to hide under their beds and ask each other what could be done to help the guards drive off this madman.

Artias, yet again looked upon as a rogue, demands that the guards listen to him.

"You have no say!" cries Unelas, running from the tavern to the group of guards. With shaking knees he stares at Janderas, saying that he will be brought to justice by the sword should he refuses to lay down his weapon. "I will not ask you again!"

"Listen to me," Artias yells and points at Gordes. "He needs a healer."

"I do not know what you mean!"

"Someone must attend to him, Unelas—he is dying!"

The guards are not yet skilled in dealing with such trouble and tremble slightly in fear of Janderas, who makes known that if Gordes dies, he will have every soul in this village beheaded. "Justice be forgotten for the day that I take your lives!"

"NO!" Unelas utters fearfully. "Take him to my house, take him there and I will attend to him."

Help

It was when his fellow needed him the most when he realized where he had to go; it was then when he understood what had to be done, and he was set—come what may.

Rushing into the Elder's house with Gordes upon his shoulders, Janderas no sooner searches for the bedroom than Unelas runs in along of Artias, showing him the way straight; and the guards come to them then, herding into the bedroom. For it is no more than a simple room with a roughly built bed, a chair and a shelf, some must stand in the doorway, observing their Elder, who tells Janderas to lay Gordes on the bed and step away to let him have a look.

At a glance Unelas knows that he has no idea what happened to Gordes.

"He has no wound, no injury of any sort—I do not know what can be done."

"What are you saying?" Artias asks, heavily worried for his friend. "That he will die?"

"I do not know."

"Then find out!" Janderas utters angrily, caring little about the guards who gathered in the room to watch him and the hunter.

"There is nothing I can do!"

To hear this takes Artias aback; nevertheless, he strikes upon an idea that could save Gordes' life. The one person who might be able to save his friend is Arianna. Tarion said she treats the wounded and the ill, so she certainly knows the art of healing. But how likely is it that she, the very woman who told him that she hates him, will help him; however, he will not take any chances and presses forth his chest and raises his head, saying with resolution that he will bring someone here to Veran to help Gordes.

"You know someone?" asks Unelas.

"Yes, but I must be quick now. Make sure he (Gordes) has all he needs. And, Unelas, you know I have never meant you or your people any harm, so attend to my friend as best as you can, or I will no more be the man I am."

"Are you threatening me?"

"No," Janderas speaks for Artias. "He merely advises you to take care of our friend. It is I who threatens you, and you do good to hear every word that I say, because if you do him wrong, oh, how great will my fury be!"

Until dawn three guards stay with Unelas to make sure no harm comes to him. Thinking of Janderas as a man who favors violence in a most savage way, they dear not leave their Elder alone.

Early in the morning Artias departs for Odas with his fellow, leaving the horses they found behind for the time being.

"We head to Odas," he tells Janderas. "Arianna, she can help."

"Arianna? That woman who treated you so shameful. She will not lift a finger to help him!"

"She must."

"She won't!"

"Then I will make her help him!"

They are both equally worried about their friend's condition and ride across the land to Odas, covering mile after mile from upon their galloping horses. Until Artias draws his animal to a halt, they stop not once.

"What is it?" asks Janderas. "Why are you stopping?"

155

"We came far, truly, but now these fine animals may graze and regain some energy."

Agreeing with a nod, Janderas points at a small glade, the smallest glade over all the land the southern forest stretches, and says that there they can pause.

While the horses feed on the blades of grass, Artias watches them with his thoughts resting on his companion's state.

"What if my fellows could have been saved?" Janderas wonders aloud.

"What do you mean?"

"You remember when you returned to Delmar with me and your kin and how I asked you later on to join me on my search for the fine horses I had lost?"

"I do, yes. Why?"

"I did so to give you time to forget all that it was that had made you be so full of ire. Traveling the land always let me feel an inner peace, and I was hoping it would give you this too. But now, to be within this realm—the creatures' realm, as you call it—fills me not with peace but guilt."

"There is no reason to feel guilty—we will save Gordes, this I pledge to you and myself."

"The understanding that our search for the horses was the reason why we found him lies heavy on me, Artias. If we wouldn't have been attacked by the claws of the forest, the horses would not have run. If not for that moment, everything would have been different. My friends would be alive; and we, we would have never left Delmar in search of the horses and never would have found Gordes, who might as well never would have been in danger.

I wonder and think and ask myself what if my companions who had been taken by the beasts that came upon us were still alive as we moved on after the fight. I wonder what if there would have been an incident that would have guided us to the beasts' dens, where I then would have found them still breathing; and I ask myself what if we would have chosen to take a different path, a safer path. How many lives could have been saved if not for a simple decision made—"

"As long as you cannot foretell the future such thoughts, as these of yours, will consume you."

"But you understand what I mean?"

"The future cannot be foretold, Janderas."

"I wish I were able to."

"But you are not, so do not trap yourself in ideas but carry on."

There is no way of knowing what lies ahead. No matter how carefully something is carried out, or how desperate a situation might appear, the outcome, the result at last, cannot be forecasted. Whether Gordes will recover, even if given Artias' pledge, is yet to be seen, just as it remains to be seen whether Arianna will assist. She might say yes but never make it to Veran, and it might be that Artias never even arrives at Odas or that he will not be leaving the village alive. Who's to say what is to come. Janderas cannot stop thinking about it, wondering what can be done to ensure safety when the unknowing is so very present.

"We should move on," he eventually says.

Feast
Of the only survivor

With struggle only the old man climbs out of the hole, trembling and swaying on reaching the house above. Lying exhausted upon the ground, breathing heavily and trembling endlessly, he looks at his hands, his shaking hands, and feels his knee, broken long ago but hurting to this day.

"Tendjan," says he, "oh, Tendjan, you — but, no, Artias is too blame, yes, only he."

Arising as quick as he can, with awkward gaze staring down into the hole, he sees all the people returning his stare and saying to him, "Get a ladder or something, just be quick; for the night, it has descended." But all the old man hears are beasts, all the critters following the sound of crying prey, sensing the feast that lies not far away.

"Get a ladder," beg the people. "Please now, get a ladder or a rope — save us."

They stare at him, ask why he is not moving, cry at him to hurry, on bended knees pledging that they do whatever he want if only he help them out. "SAVE US!"

And he then vanishes from their sight, leaving them behind in the hole, from the bottom of which they continue to stare up, hoping that he return with a ladder or a rope.

"Where are you?" they call. "Please, say something!"

Steps trudge upon the ground above and they call his name, say that they though he had left them to die, though to them comes not their fellow; they see the face of a beast arising, staring with slobbering maw down at them.

At once it comes upon them, leaping into the whole, its claws hitting into the flesh of whomever it sets upon. Within this hole, barely larger than the house above, not one of these souls can escape the beast, and more come to join the feast. The people try to climb up, try to escape, to shield themselves even with each other or their beloveds while witnessing the beasts tearing their fellows apart. Seized and brought out of the hole to feed the young waiting above, some of these souls are to die a most horrible death. The hole fills with limps, organs, and corpses showing bone beneath ripped flesh while throughout this slaughter, the old man tries to hide in the undergrowth, only glimpsing at all the critters joining in the killing. Each bark and growl, each cry and wail awakens him to what he has done, and he closes his ears with his hands and presses his face into the soil, vomiting.

Until dawn he hears the creatures eating or fighting with each other over prey; and then, when the sun has risen, he ascends a tree with enough branches to make him part from the ground into height, where he waits for the last beast to leave; nevertheless, even as every man-eater has left, he remains upon the tree, not ever bold enough to leave his shelter. For at least two days he will stay here, thinking only about Artias, who must die for what he has forced him and his people into doing.

To Face the Truth

The truth of the village's existence came to light; and he could see, in whole, the vile purpose behind the lie, and it dawned on him just how little fellowship there had been between him and others.

Some may say, "Wandering this land would not be so difficult if it weren't for the wildlife"; unfortunately, this is incorrect, simply: one can quickly lose orientation and end up dead or adrift. For those who often range the land, however, the mountains, stars and winds help them find direction. Skilled in this field, these experienced travelers almost never come off their way; and among them is Artias, who has a magnificent sense of direction as well, which makes it even easier for him and his companion to reach Odas, regardless of the lush vegetation which can arouse confusion as to where lies the way.

They see Odas shortly before sundown, with foreboding riding into forlorn grounds. In sight of this forsaken place on Earth, Janderas dismounts his horse and strides through the village, trying to understand why it appears to have been abandoned.

"Where is everyone?" he wonders, looking at Artias.

"Something does not feel right."

Upon leaping down his horse, Artias hears a sound as made by treading upon a twig and forthwith tells Janderas to listen.

"This place is a bane," Janderas mutters nonetheless. "Not ever would I want to live he—"

"Be still now!"

After a moment of listening for movement in the foliage, the hunter turns to face his horse. To see this mare's tranquil look gives him little reason to fear an attack; but even so, he remains calm and whispers only as he tells his friend, "She (the mare) is calm, so we certainly are not about to face any of the claws of the forest. We should stay wary nevertheless."

"Well, she does not hear quite well, Artias, but as you say. Let's see if someone's home."

Straight approaching the nearest house, Janderas bangs his fist against the door, demanding that whomever inside open up.

"Our friend is dying," says he. "We are here to summon assistance. Open up at once, I say!"

Nobody opens, not now nor after a while.

A last time he says, "Open up or I shall," and then, no instant later, breaches the door with drawn blade, crying into the house, "Come here to me wherever you are!"

"What are you doing!" Artias strides over to the house, taking a look inside. "Janderas."

"There is nobody here," says his fellow, returning from a room near the front door.

"I do not have to kick in a door to tell; and if I had to break-in, then I would not do it so recklessly. You even scared the horses for a moment!"

"Whoever's here shall show himself; we have no time to spare waiting!" Janderas roams his eyes over the interior, shouting, "You hear, come out of your hiding now!"

"My fellow, I know we must hurry, but you should not announce our presence 'til—"

"They are strange people anyway. Listen here to me, Artias, some of them were glaring at us while we were escorting them. Would you glare at your saviors? No, you wouldn't, because you would be glad to be alive. I say, they always struck me as an awkward bunch, yet I—foolish as

I was — believed you to be the reason for their behavior."

"Glaring you say? That does sound quite strange indeed."

"I advise that we take a look around," says Janderas; "perhaps they are here, hiding from us, unwilling to help us!"

"Yes, we should, but let us do so quietly."

"I cannot kick in a door quietly!"

"I don't think you want to have a beast on your tail, Janderas. Who knows what we will find."

"Fine, all right."

Artias returns to his horse and pats it on the shoulder. He can't help to feel watched, observed by someone or something and advises his companion to be wary and "Do not separate."

Someone approaches him then, a man of great age whose name is Tarion; and he, with unbound fury, comes rushing out of the bushes with a knife, charging blindly at Artias in whom he sees the reason for all the trouble.

"WATCH OU!" cries Janderas. "BEHIND YOU!"

Tarion blusters and snorts, scaring the horses on trying to stab down Artias and bashes straight into the kick of a hoofed mare, a kick of such force that he is cast through the air before he hits upon the ground.

Squealing his pain, Tarion tries to rise, swaying at his ever move.

"Where are the others?" Janderas withdraws from the door, walking at a swift pace to the old man on the ground. "Speak now or never again!"

"All w-was good … it was all good b-before you c-came!"

"We need to speak to Arianna," Artias utters most fiercely, grabbing the knife and flinging it away into the forest. As confused as he is disgusted at the sight of Tarion's bloodstained clothes, he threatens: "Tell me where she is, or I will forget myself and let you lie wounded!"

"You wa-want to see her? Well ... hah, sadly, t-that is not possible." Tarion feels just how severely the horse injured him—death is close, coming to him at his ever word.

"Where is she, Tarion? I shall not ask you again!"

"One day, one day y-you will feel a knife driving down, down i-into your, your throat. Laugh, that I will. So ver-very loud I, I shall laugh. Curse you. Yes, yes. I curse you! You and you all there! See me, me laughing at your de-death!"

Artias does not recognize Tarion anymore; the menacing tone in his voice is frightening, letting this old man appear more like a scoundrel than a settler, a wounded one who manages to find the strengths to rave in such pain.

"Where is she?" Artias urges him to answer the question. "And where are the others?"

"I am very well aware o-of you, Artias. O-oh, yes, yes, yes, I a-am."

"I vow I will let you lie—"

"Your o-oh so brave strive to h-have every village h-hemmed in is depriving me—us, us—of, of f-fare.

Say, Ar-Artias, did you ever wonder w-why Arianna's house is, is not among the o-others? You know you did, b-because you asked me about it. S-shall I say ... where else to cut flesh and have a f-feast."

Neither Artias nor Janderas says a word. Although they assume to know what Tarion is saying, they shudder at the very thought.

"Gilgaron and Tindras s-should have dealt with you in the forest, b-but, no … as it appears—ah, w-we both know what, what happened, don't we?"

"No, Gilgaron and Tindras were honest and—"

"And what? Good-hearted? Do you really think they follow you after you killed Beras o-only because of a pledge or, or vow? No, Artias, they simply thought you n-need to be dealt with! Helping us with the creature … no, no Artias, you did n-not. How long till you would have f-found out! I—we—c-couldn't take the risk, not since you s-stayed in her house… her house overnight. You, you shouldn't… h-ha-ha-ave stayed in her ho-ho-use, Artias."

With disgust looking at Tarion's bloody garment, Janderas spits down on him, saying: "A corpse-eater he is, a cannibal. I tell you, he ate the others—he and whoever else is with him."

"Gilgaron, Tindras, yes even Ardegan were my kin," Tarion says, in unending pain continuing shouting that he knew Artias means trouble by the moment he had asked him why Arianna's house is quite the distance away from Odas, and he says, "E-every now, now and then, we, w-we ha-have to cut up our meal and f-feast. How, how e-easy do you think it is to, to, to keep everyone well-feed 'til to, to be feed on?"

"YOU FOUL FLESH-EATER," cries Janderas, but Tarion states that they ate only the dead 'til the first stockade was built and forced them to ensure their survival no more by claiming to burry the dead (whereas they ate them) but by killing. "B-because of you, Artias, we needed to settle here, call people here, fatten them, kill them to eat them. O-only b-because of y-you and yo-your stockades we ha-have become murderers!

O-oh, blessed be the day you came here. F-forget the creature, our chance to get rid of, of you, y-yes, o-our chance arose. But, yes, you b-became a risk before you even dealt with, with the beast."

"Tarion," Artias utters anxiously, "where are the others?"

"There is only I left."

"I do not believe you. You can yet decide to walk a path of honor and tell me where the others are?"

"S-say, Janderas, why d-do you not, not tell your fellow of the beasts, the beasts that a-attacked us?"

"I already have," says Janderas, with revulsion looking at Tarion, whom he was regarding as a poor, old soul until a moment ago, when all his compassion began to turn into disgust, arousing an ache for this man's death.

"And yet you stand with him."

"Hush your mouth and tell us where the others are!"

"Look around, Janderas, d-do you, you see them any-anywhere?"

"I will not ask you again," Janderas shouts, approaching the old man with drawn blade, ready to kill him here and now if he does not answer the question. "I shall have you."

"Sooner or later, s-sooner or—"

"NO," Artias yells as he sees how his friend dashes at Tarion and drives the blade through his gut.

Urging the blade through all the bones in the way, Janderas cries as he tears his sword out of the body and thrusts it into Tarion's throat. In his rage he looks down at the old man's dead body, spitting at the corpse, with disgust saying, "I shall not hear a word you say!"

"Why did you do that?" hollers Artias. "Why on earth did you do that?"

Wordlessly Janderas steps away from the body and looks at the two horses.

"I will never eat you," says he to them, "neither one of you."

"Listen, Janderas, I will go to Arianna's house now and see whether she's there, and you, you stay here and watch the horses."

"No, we go together."

"Just wait!" utters Artias and leaves his friend alone with the animals. "I know the way, so just wait here," he says before vanishing among trees...

But when he returns, striding quickly towards his horse, he tells Janderas nothing more than to mount his. There is not a single word he says besides of this, which appears very odd to his companion as Artias is no man who keeps secrets.

"What is going on?" Janderas insists on knowing what the hunter found in Arianna's house.

"Nothing!"

"Nothing?"

"Yes, nothing besides of an underground chamber and bodies and blood and—listen, let's just go."

"What are you saying, Artias?"

"That I wish to depart from this horrid place."

"You know what I am asking you!"

"They are all dead, all right! Everyone is dead!"

"You tell me Tarion killed everyone?"

"As far as I could tell"—Artias tries to withstand the urge to vomit—"he might have."

"That foul being!"

"I could not see that chamber the first time I was in her house; for the fireplace, it covers the entrance. I did not even know she had a basement. But, but she does, and she has—so that is why he did not want me to make fire. Yes, yes, now I see. 'Have some trust in us,' said he. All that he said, deceiving me!"

"What exactly did you find?"

"A hole underneath her house, a chamber that can be entered through the fireplace, and therein I could see bones scattered over bloody soil!

You ask me, yes, yes, I believe Tarion killed them. I believe he lured the people to her house to let beasts have a feast; and he then, at sunrise, feed on their remains." (Artias may believe to be right, but if only he would know what really happened ... .)

"A dreadful thought," utters Janderas. "I say, are you sure what you are—"

"I AM!" (Artias should not hold his verdict in certainty but be open to doubt. He does not question his conclusion, however; overwhelmed with abhorrence, he desires to leave above all else.)

"Okay, all right, calm yourself," says Janderas. "This event frightens me as much as it frightens you."

"Let's—just let us go, Janderas."

"We need her!"

"There is nobody here!"

"Maybe she is hiding in one of the houses!"

"No, she isn't, Janderas."

"We must be sure."

Together they begin to check the houses, searching for any sign of Arianna.

All the homes of the people Artias looked upon as simple settlers appear differently now that he knows for what diabolic reason they were (kept) here, and he starts to think about Arianna and how she held her boy when he entered her house.

He can only imagine that she was forced into submission by Tarion and his kin yet struggles greatly with thinking of Gilgaron, who welcomed him so friendly in his home; Tindras, who was willing to help him come what may; Ardegan, whose courage he admired (for Artias knew was no warrior and yet acted so bravely) as men whose aim was to keep safe not their fellowmen but their fare from being taken. It is strange nevertheless that Arianna said she loved Ardegan. Her tears seemed real and her grief just as much.

"Artias," he is then called by Janderas. "There is nobody anywhere but quite many inhuman footprints."

"Can you imagine how that is like, to be in a chamber underground without a way to escape the beasts you hear prowling about just above your head. How much fear must these people have felt as it dawned on them for what sinister reason they were in her house...

"The footprints are all over, Artias. I—"

...and then he emerges to feed on the dead, on the remains of the dead. He emerged to feed on the people he once knew. Those he laughed and smiled with; those he cried and grieved with; those he drunk and spoke with and probably also promised something he feed on."

"Artias," Janderas shouts at him, seizing his friend by the arm, "listen to me! We must leave this place, and that quickly."

Assuming that certain critters, primarily lone predators, could have hidden some of the bodies to supply their litter with fare for some time, he urges his friend to "get on to your horse" and mounts his straight.

Artias, however great his abhorrence, awakes to the fall of twilight. At once getting on to his horse, he rides off, heading for Veran with Janderas.

Love and hate
He inquired of her the truth but was told less than he had sought to know.

However often the horses need to graze and rest, it is to their doing only that Artias and Janderas can cover a great distance within a single day. It is said, "Journeying on horseback is the traveler's joy." Right now, though, neither Artias nor Janderas can rejoice in traveling by horseback. Worried and troubled, they ride in mutual silence, trying to see a way to help their friend. Though Gordes' fate hinges upon their success, it seems as if they were to carry misfortune; and what they have discovered in Odas lies heavy on them, and preys on their minds withal.

It takes time 'til one of them says something than has nothing to do with the essentials of survival.

Ashamed of himself, Janderas tells Artias that he failed to ward the righteous.

"I tried, truly I tried to be brave," says he, "but even so I failed."

"Why do you—"

"Did you know that I ventured to Arjovan on my own?"

"How could I."

"I tell you, Artias, I had to wander across foreign countries, across the grounds of the wicked to reach Arjovan.

There were gibbets, Artias, beside me, ahead of me, all over bounding the road to horrid places. I saw people who were whipped, caged, and thrown into lakes; and others who had been battered half dead and left to die in the gutter. Never before in my life had I seen such savageness; but I turned around, kept shut my eyes, and went on my way: I cared not to help, for I was afraid, too afraid to act, too scared to even think of what might befall me if I dared to.

Throughout my voyage, Artias, I had come across people who needed help, even cried at me for help, but I could not move, not act. Guilt is a strong feeling, a feeling that has been accompanying me for so long now. It drove me to strive for justice, justice that should have had its beginning here in Arjovan. But I have failed; I have failed to ward off evil; I failed. Yes, I failed."

"I have heard of such places, my fellow, but whatever you have been through there, whatever has happened there, it let you be the man you are today; and as I see it, you are through and through a righteous soul."

Janderas halts at once and stares down at the ground, saying that he was wrong "and a fool to think I could ever change anything. It will never be, because it can never be. Perhaps it shall never be how it should be."

He was sure he could one day speak of Arjovan as (the) Land of Beast and Man where there be no love for those foul in heart; apparently, his wholehearted desire to attain this has been crumbling since he left Odas.

"I should not have assisted the people of that wicked place, Artias. I should have simply left them to their fate. It would not have been a barbaric one, then."

"It would have been wrong to let them die, simply."

"Yes, that is so—say, do you think Arianna was among the dead?"

"I could not tell."

"Maybe she is alive."

"If so, then I do not care; I must find a way to help Gordes now. Our friend, he must be—"

"Unelas does not know what to do!" states Janderas.

"Yes, but perhaps we can take Gordes to Delmar, or treat him in Veran as best as we can."

"We? I am not familiar with the art of healing. My wife, your sister, she is, but taking him to Delmar might not be possible."

"It is too far away, I know."

"So do you know what can be done?"

"I am yet thinking of a solution."

Janderas is quiet on seeing Veran through the leafage. Hoping that Gordes is alive, he quickens his horse's pace and rides at a gallop out into the glade, thereupon discovering that the horses they chose to leave in Veran are grazing in the glade under guard. He slows down, drawing nearer to them at a canter. A step away from the men watching the horses, he halts and asks, "Are they well?"

"They are," says one of the men, trembling slightly to see Janderas, who threatened the guards so savagely that his face will never be forgotten.

"Have they been groomed?"

"Of course," says the man.

"Good! Watch them careful—"

"Come now," says Artias, riding by.

At once Janderas follows his companion into Veran, dismounting his horse right away upon arriving at the Elder's house. Without knocking they enter and stride to the bedroom, where Gordes is no more.

"Where is he?" wonders Artias, fearing for his friend. "It can't be that he is—no."

Before they can leave the house in search of the Elder, whom Janderas vows to question about their missing friend, someone comes in and treads heavily to the kitchen.

"Dare if anything came to him," mutters Janderas and leaves the bedroom, shouting, "Come here to me Elder, and that be at once!"

But it is not the Elder who wished to search the kitchen for a drink 'til hearing Janderas' shouting.

"Gordes!" Artias utters, delighted.

"Artias!" Gordes utters, delighted.

Staring at the hunter, only able to recall the moment he heard Artias' voice after venturing for many days, he says, "My friend, I thought I would never see you again!"

"You had us worried, Gordes—heavily worried. We did not know whether you would make it through."

"I heard you calling my name, though I was certain I would die—my strength had left me and my legs, they could only just keep me straight."

"Circumstances were in good fortune," says Janderas. "If it weren't for the horses' flight, then well ... ."

Gordes eyes fall on Janderas and he says to him, "I remember that we parted ways."

"As I said, circumstances were in—"

"Wait! Where is Hentario?"

And silence descends over his fellows, making known the tragedy without words; and Gordes lowers his head, asking almost silently, "How (his friend died)?"

"His skull was—"

"Who did it, Artias? Who?"

"You know who!"

"Which one of them kill my friend, Artias? Who was it? Tell me now!"

"We fell upon every bandit we found dwelling in that rotten cave," Janderas declares, saying thereupon that whoever of these fiends had run from the fight were pursued and slain.

For a while they remain in silence, reminiscing about the days they had been traveling with their friends. Back then, theses days seemed to never end. Today, only the memory is left. "But say, when did you awake?"

"Not very long ago. Oh, how very sweet was the face looking at me!"

"What?" Janderas gapes at Artias, thinking Gordes means Unelas. "Who exactly treated you?"

"A woman. Arianna is her name. My future wife she will be. Yes."

In utter silence Artias steps away from Gordes, pacing up and down.

"What is going on here?" he asks himself; and so does Janderas, who wastes no time on finding out and straight asks Gordes where she is. "Tell me where that witch is at!"

"How dare you call her that!"

"Silence now," demands Artias and calmly asks Gordes if he knows where she is.

"I must speak to her," he says, "urgently."

"She should be here in—"

Gordes looks at the front door, hushing as Unelas steps in and gapes worriedly at Janderas, whom he sees as a ruffian.

At once approached by the hunter, Unelas steps back a pace in fear of what may follow.

"I could have put your friend behind bars," he says, "but I did not—I treated him fairly. No harm came to him as you can see!"

"Calm yourself, Unelas, I wish to thank you and ask you where Arianna is?"

"She will be here shortly to make sure your frien—hold up now, I say. From where do you know my daughter?"

"Are you speaking of Arianna? She is your daughter? Arianna is your daughter?"

"Yes."

"That can't be!" grumbles Janderas.

"She struck me as a woman whose only family was her son," says Artias.

"Well, that isn't so! Now, Artias, tell me from where you know her?"

"From Odas."

"She does not live in Odas, Artias!"

"Perhaps I am mistaking her. Please, can I see her?"

"As I said, she will be here shortly."

The hunter wishes to ask the Elder whether he and Janderas could have something to drink, for the travel was a long one, when Gordes insists that he tell him what happened while he was out cold.

"I will tell you everything in due course, my fellow."

"No, Artias, you tell me now!"

"I will in due course, Gordes. I am glad you are alive. By all that I treasure, your live means so much to me, so do not treat me as if I were your servant and be patien—"

Arianna's sudden arrival brings the dialogue to an abrupt end; and as she joins the group, approaching Artias with caution and bewilderment, she seems to worry about what he may say because of the things she told him, yet before Artias can utter a word, she asks him if she could talk to him.

"I wanted to ask you the same," he agrees and ask Janderas to join them. Arianna does not want to speak to anyone else than to Artias, though, and so only he leaves the house with her after telling his fellows that he will be back shortly.

Night is approaching while he walks with her through Veran, not once looking at the people around.

"Unelas is my father, Artias, but I beg of you not to tell him where I lived."

"He already knows."

"You told him?"

"I could not believe that you are here in Veran. Listen, Arianna, I was in Odas, know what that village was about, for what purpose it was built, so you must no longer choose your words with caution."

"You know? Everything?"

"Yes, but even so, open questions remain. Tell me, Arianna, do you, how shall I say—"

"Eat flesh?"

"Yes."

"Never I have. My father, he built my house. He wanted us—me and him—to live there, but the nights can be so dark in the forest that he chose to raise me elsewhere. He chose to built another house here in the glade. As you can see, out of one became many."

"What about Odas?"

"My son, he was not my son, but his mother lay dead in the forest. I found him crying near her body. That is when I first met Beras and his kind. They, they were eating her when I came. I tried to run away with the boy, but I could not outrun them. To the house, built by my own father, they took me, forced me and the child on the ground, and wanted to—I dare not remember that day, Artias."

Knowing that it must be hard for her to speak of something that, without doubt, changed her very being, Artias feels sorry but must nevertheless know what happened.

"I beg of you to tell me—what I saw, it was not, I cannot forget."

"They could not kill a child, Artias, okay! That is why I had to stay there. 'But only until he grow old,' they said.

They began to built houses and a tavern, and the tribes they came by on their daily searches for dead bodies in the woods were asked to help them built. These traveling tribes, every member of them, thought they found a home at last, a home that they will have raised. No home, a place to live until to be slain and eaten."

"I thought they ate the bodies they ought to burry—"

"What? Don't ask of me to remember such things, I beg of you!"

"I did not mean to—"

"I don't want to remember!"

"Arianna, did you never think about running away?"

"Of course I did, but I did not know where to go, how to get away. I have once tried to flee, but Beras, though he always was so kind to me despite his nature, told me that he would find me anywhere, because he knows where to look. I did not know what he meant, but it terrified me.

Listen, Artias, if I could have run away, I would have; but then they began to dig a hole under my house and came together to eat and," and then she sinks to her knees, crying out her misery. However kindly she was treated by them, she always knew, one day, she will end up dead, just like all the wounded or ill who had come to her in hopes of being treated for their pains. And Artias, as loving as he is, believes her, for he believes to see the truth and only the truth (nothing but *her* truth).

"To this day, Artias, to this day I can hear them screams. Beras and Gilgaron, they have once told me that they were forced to do this. I did not believe 'em. No, they—if not for Ardegan, I would probably be dead already."

"Why? Tarion sai—"

"Do not speak of him. Tarion, he was the worst of them all."

"Arianna, you told me you loved Ardegan, but he was Tarion's kin."

"He was the only one who would protect me, the only one who never told me to mind my words. He was there for me, and though I hate myself for feeling as I do, I love him, and when he was gone, who would be there for me? Who would protect me and my boy? No, Artias, I cannot say that I do not hate you; because I do, although I should not, because you have no fault."

Artias lays his hand on her shoulder, telling every person coming by that she grieves for the death of a friend. Many of those who see her pain wish to help her but are not allowed to; she tells them all to begone and that they shall not care about her, because she is not worth their love.

"It's okay, Arianna," says Artias. "You have no fault, either."

"You have no idea. I hoped you would find that horrid chamber while waiting for the beast. You did not, and I did not tell you. I was afraid, so afraid, so terrified of Tarion and his kin, and I am so sorry for feeling as I do!"

"It's okay. Say, you found your way to Veran alone?"

"Yes, with luck, but—I don't want to speak anymore. Just leave me."

It is more than clear to Artias that she will run into the woods and call every beast near and far to take her live should he dare to leave her alone now. She lives through the ordeal of her life every night and day.

"I won't leave you," says he and helps her rise, saying thereupon that they should go back to Unelas and his fellows, and he tells her that she can join him and the others on their travels if she likes.

"No," she stutters. "I can see how your friend looks at me, with disgust!"

"I assume you mean Janderas. I say, he will do so no more once I will have told him your story—he has a good heart."

But Arianna does not want to join them; she hates Artias, and that with all her heart.

An Honest Promise
If it had not been for his loving words, she would have had herself be slain — so at least it seemed to him.

Artias and his two companions sit at a table together with Arianna and her father, waiting painterly for dawn, when they will take their leaving. Gordes, however, says that he would like to stay, much to Artias' delight, but Janderas does not share his friend's pleasure and asks Gordes why he wants to settle down.

"I decided to marry." Gordes speaks with bliss in his heart anytime he looks at Arianna.

"Who says I'll marry you?" she asks, astonished. It never dawned on her just how deeply she has touched his heart. Love at first sight, but "I do not want to marry you?"

"I am a fine man, strong and loving."

"Are you?" says Unelas doubtfully. "Who says I allow you to —"

"Allow me to?" Arianna rises from her chair, scowling at her father. "I do not need your consent, father!"

"I just say that —"

"That I must ask you."

"No, not you — *he*."

"He mustn't, either."

"But —"

"No, father, it would be my decision!"

In rage Unelas stares at Gordes, promising him that if ever he treats her unfairly or raises his hand against her, he will no longer be a peaceful man and kill him.

"Never would I raise my hand against a woman," utters Gordes. "Never!"

"I will not marry you!" Arianna declares and wants to leave to hear no more of Gordes' elusions as Artias asks her if she rather be alone or with someone who shares her pain, for Gordes himself is in pain.

"Why is everyone speaking as if I were not here?" grumbles Unelas, leaning back in his chair. His eyes focus on his daughter only as he tells her, "Arianna, my daughter, I thought you were dead until you suddenly stand on my doorstep, so forgive me if all I want is to see you happy," and he then looks at Gordes, saying, "If she is happy with you, then so be it; but if she does not want to have you on her side, then you must accept that."

"Well," Gordes gets up from his chair, pressing forth his chest, "I would like to stay here in Veran nevertheless. I will be of great assistance to your guards; and maybe, one day hopefully, your daughter will look at me the same way I look on her."

"You can stay," Unelas agrees, "but I will keep my eye on you."

"You shall not regret."

"I am sure—"

"Who says I'll stay," Arianna yells at Gordes with (and this should strike Artias as rather peculiar) a frown of contempt. "Maybe I will leave—alone."

"I go where you go," Gordes announces at once.

"You cannot!"

"Oh, I can. My heart is yours to my dying day; and I say, wherever you go, I will go, and if that means I must face death."

In tears Arianna dashes out of the house, at once followed by Gordes, whose worries for the love of his life make him run faster than ever; and as he catches up with her, seizing her by the arm to draw her to a halt, he asks what he said that made her cry.

"I did not mean to offend you," says he. "You may believe I am no good man, but in truth I am a fine one, and will do what I can to make you see this."

And she snivels and turns around, acting most strangely then, for although she seems to cry, she smirks beyond his sight.

Awakening
In the water of a pond they found a knife, knowing from the blade's telling that vengeance was or still is desired by its owner.

Janderas is riding to Delmar alongside of Artias and with seven horses in tow, sometimes brooding over Gordes' decision to stay in Veran.

"I never thought I would miss someone I never really knew," he grunts.

"What do you mean?" asks Artias, slowing down his horse to dismount the animal and let it graze.

"Gordes, I mean Gordes." Joining Artias side, Janderas watches the horses feed on the green, wishing Gordes would be here with them. "I never thought I would miss his company this much."

"Neither did I. The first time we met, you were, well, let's say rough."

"Do you think she'll marry him?"

"Let's say, I hope he finds what he looks for."

"And what about us?"

"Well, maybe we should marry, too."

"What are you saying, Artias! Dare you ask a married man such a—"

"It was joking, Janderas."

"… I know."

"Sure you did."

"Yes, I knew."

"Okay, yes, you did know. But, seriously now, I think when we're in Delmar, it might be time for me to settle down, too."

"No more travels?"

In thought Artias stares at the sky, thinking aloud, "That must have been why. Of course, yes."

"What are you talking about now?"
"I was thinking about Odas and—"
"Forget that forsaken place!"
"I cannot, because I cannot understand why the people were brought away from there, although, well, you know for what it was built."
"You could have asked Arianna why."
"She would not say."
"Find comfort in the thought that justice has been served, Artias."
"Yes, but—"
"I don't want to hear of it!"
"Do you not desire to know why someone who eats his fellows guides them out into the wilds?"
"Obviously for a sinister reason, or it was because of the beast at last."
"I do not think the beast had anything to do with it. I mean, they returned to Odas."
"Yes, they did, because I brought them there."
"It does not make any sense."
"Artias, I did not want to tell you this, but now I have to, despite how foolish I feel about saying it: I told them whatever beast you had summoned would vanish at your death."
"You do not really believe in such things, do you?"
"What kinds of things? Sorcery?"
"Yes."
"Well, I believed them their story, so what do you think."
"I think your sudden emergence hindered Tarion from carrying out his plan."
"You know what I think?
"No—what?"
"That you think too much."
"Janderas, I merely try to understand."

"Understand what, that he persuaded everyone to leave by a lie, probably promising them a better life elsewhere, at just some place where no beast speaker will endanger them."

"What if he wanted to take them to others, and with others I mean others like him. Obviously I was a problem, so why stay at place I might return to and discover his doings at last. I am sure that is how it was. Say, can you show me where you first encountered them."

"Tell me you are joking!"

"No, I am not, Janderas. So, can you show me?"

"Yes, I can."

"Is it far."

"No, it's actually rather close by. Given how quickly we reached them, I would say it's but a leap away."

"We who?"

"Me and my fellows, Artias. We were preparing to rest here in this glade when we heard people calling for help. I told you about that at our first encounter."

"You say that was here."

"No, I don't say, I know."

"Well, there is no need to rush if it is as close as you say, but I would prefer that we hurry."

"Sure as if I had nothing better to do. I have a wife waiting for me, you know."

"I know, and forgive me that I ask you to help me, my fellow, yet I do require your assistance — please, assist me."

"I did not say I wouldn't."

Janderas takes the hunter to a pond partly cloaked in the forest's lush greenery. That a fight took place here cannot be seen by the untrained eye: too many recently passing creatures obscured the signs of the fight. If it weren't for Artias' skills in reading tracks, developed and sharpened during years of living out in the open (and not at last being conscious of the event itself), he would not be able to see that something odd occurred here.

Dismounting the mare at once, he inspects the ground and the broken twigs, looking at the footprints in the mud and the earth beyond, and then he looks at Janderas, informing him, "I do not think that there is a cave anywhere near—"

"So now we are looking for a cave, or what?"

"No, you are not listening."

"Perhaps you should enlighten me, then!"

"Either there is another village like Odas somewhere here, of which I am sure; or whomever the people Tarion tried to reach live in a cave, which I doubt, because all the footprints of creatures are such of beasts living not in dens nor in caves."

"I see, but I do not think we will find a village here."

"We should look out for a man-made structure—it must not necessarily be a village. It might as well be a house or a hut or—"

"You know how ridiculous that sounds. Artias, you were the one warning everyone of beasts of prey, saying a stockade is needed to survive, and now you say we should look out for a hut."

"Or a house, yes."

"That's odd."

"Just keep your eyes open, my fellow."

From upon his horse Janderas has a far better view of the surrounding environment than his friend and can look over the low-growing bushes, several feet ahead.

"I wonder what I am hoping to see," says he, looking around. "We are days away from any village. Listen, Artias, every men of Odas is dead besides of Arianna, so wouldn't interrogating her be more effective than searching for a hut or village while having all these horse with us."

"I don't know if everyone is dead—maybe someone survived."

"All right, all right. I say, we should have a look around, see if we find anything interesting around the pond."

"Say, do you see anything from up on your horse?"

"Nothing of interest."

"Are you sure?"

"I'll have another look around. Maybe you will find something meanwhile."

"Yes, maybe—"

Artias hushes and treads into the pond, trying to see what he descried glittering under the surface of the water. There lies a knife, an old rusty knife that shows an engraved name as he raises it out of the wanter.

"Janderas," he summons his friend and hands him the knife. "You see the engraved name?"

"Surjes. Who's that?" Janderas wonders, returning the knife.

"Doesn't sound familiar to me."

"If it is a name, then it means the blade is meant for someone!"

"How is that to be understood?"

"How long must you have been wandering this land and helping people that you forgot what a name on a blade means."

"Just tell me, Janderas."

"Vengeance. The name on the blade says whose heart the blade is to be thrust into. Surjes is obviously someone who is wanted dead, or has been slain already, but that must not necessarily have anything to do with all of this—there are many people who seek vengeance, you know."

"We must find out whose knife this is."

"I do not think you will have any luck finding out—could be anyone's from here to the end of the known lands."

"Well, whoever it is, they must have been here, here in Arjovan, here at this pond, where we are standing just now."

"You are chasing ghosts, Artias. Did it ever strike you that the beast could have been the actual cause of the people's leaving—to me, that's the most obvious reason."

"If so, then tell me why they returned with you and even decided to stay there after you and your men had left?"

"I cannot say I know why, besides of repeating what I have said already."

"Something is not right, Janderas. Perhaps Arianna knows more."

"If I were you, I would go home—"

"I am not out of my mind, Janderas!"

"A little deaf you are. I am advising that you ask your kin. Surjes could be someone they know of."

"If so, you would recognize the name, too—I am sure it would sound familiar to you."

"Really?" Asking for the knife, Janderas takes another look at the name, suddenly saying: "Oh, yes, of course, now I know."

"You know whose knife this is?"

"Yes, obviously, it is a stranger's."

"Can you stop making fun of me."

"Oh, come on, Artias. Do you not somehow feel like if you search for something where there is nothing!"

"No!"

"All right. Listen here: Let's ask Arianna and Unelas; and Gordes, he might know something. We can ask around Veran, make inquiries. If left without a trace, we head for Delmar and see from there on—but if we do not discover anything, then let it rest."

"You know I cannot do that."

"Yes, I thought so."

Inquiry
Wondering whose knife they had found, they asked around, but were as blind to the lies told unto them as they were to the owner's masquerade.

Dark clouds cast a gloom over the land and keep away the Sun's rays, and showers of rain fall upon the earth, sending streams of water through the glade. The rainstorm is sudden and violent, preventing the stouthearted men and women in Veran from working on the stockade.

Artias and Janderas arrive at Veran when the storm comes upon the land with such severity that it floods parts of the grassland, forcing them both to hurry to the stable to shelter their animals. There they find a man who's taking care of the other fair horses while, not often, glaring at the sky. As if it be trying to immerse the land, the storm's strength grows gradually, letting every soul in Veran struggle to keep their homes dry.

"I never saw it rain so heavily," says the man upon looking at Janderas' horse, patting it gently on the neck.

"Indeed, the *Sky's falls** is heavy."

The man—not of great strength or endurance but kind and warmhearted, with nothing more than a shirt underneath a wide vest to hide his belly—assures that the horses are in good hands.

"I am sure they are," says Artias on leaping down his horse and handing the man the rein, thereupon asking whether the name Surjes sounds familiar to him. "We found a knife that might be his."

"A knife?"

"Yes."

"Is his name on the blade or the hilt?"

"The blade."

"Oh!"

"Well, do you know a man—"

"Who seeks vengeance will never be at peace."

"No, you misunderstand," Janderas explains. "We try to find out more about an incident. The knife belongs to neither one of us. We found it."

Unfortunately, the man cannot help them: he knows neither who Surjes is nor whom might.

"I wish I were able to help you," says he, removing the bridles and saddles.

At a quick pace Janderas leaves the stable with his companion, stopping not once until reaching the Elder's house. Upon knocking, Gordes opens the door, looking surprised to see his fellows again.

"You two never cease to amaze!" says he, summoning Unelas as he steps aside to let them in.

Standing in the doorway, for Artias thinks it is not on Gordes to decide whether they may enter, he waits with Janderas 'til the Elder comes forth, with bemused gaze, treading heavily to them.

Saying to both of them, "Step in now," Unelas takes a look outside before slamming close the door, assuming the cloudburst to have caused their return.

"You are drenched," says he on seeing how soaked they are. "Quick, off your clothes before death catches you."

Unelas vanishes in his bedroom, shortly after returning with Arianna and fresh clothes for both of his visitors.

"Wear these until yours are dry," he says, handing them both fine clothes of braided leather.

One after the other vanishes into the bedroom and returns freshly dressed and with a smile.

"Thank you," Artias utters gratefully. "I am sorry for troubling you so often, though once more I must talk to you—to all of you."

"What about?" asks Gordes; and "So you haven't come to seek shelter from the storm?" says Unelas, proceeding in thought: "I wonder what is going on in these two men's heads?"

"Say, does any one of you know someone who goes by the name Surjes?"

"No," Gordes says; and "no," Unelas says; but "yes," says Arianna.

"Who is he?" asks Janderas.

"I do not know. I merely heard Ardegan mentioning that name once to Tarion. What about they spoke, that I do not know; but Tarion, he seemed frightened."

"Might be that they knew whose striving for vengeance," mentions Janderas.

"Vengeance?" wonders Gordes and asks his fellows why they speak of vengeance.

"The name is engraved on a blade," the hunter informs him, keen on hearing what he may say about this.

"I see," is what Gordes says. "Whoever's it is, those who want vengeance strike at whomever they believe is hindering them from their seek. I know, I was like that myself once upon a time. Of course, now no more, for a lovely flower showed me—"

"Enough," Arianna grumbles. "You were all day long dancing around me—please, do stop."

"My heart, it does not allow me to."

"Can we please focus!" Janderas, though taking joy in seeing how Gordes approaches Arianna, thinks that now time is not to be wasted on flattering. "Artias needs your help, so help him!"

Looking at Unelas, he continues, asking, "May we inquiry about that name here in Veran?"

"You may."

"Good. We shall do so as soon as the weath—"

"We cannot wait," Artias says and tells Gordes and the others that he and Janderas will be back before they embark upon a journey he cannot doubt to be necessary to find the man they seek, and then he leaves again.

Standing in the rain and hearing the front door of a house dry and warm closing, Janderas looks down at the fresh clothes he has just been given.

"Wet yet again," grunts he.

"Do not be so tidy."

"I do not like to be drenched."

"Neither you nor I, my friend."

They go from door to door, asking whoever's home whether they know of a man named Surjes.

"No," most of the people say, although there is one among the many who can tell them something more than merely stating it an odd name. He says, "Sounds like a name from the north."

"Why from the north?"

"I ... never heard a name beginning with *Sur* until I was in the northern parts of the Sun (Arjovan)."

"My kin are from the northern plain," Artias thinks aloud, unintentionally making the man assume he speaks to him.

"Well, I just say that Surjes sounds, well, strange."

"Forgive me, I was thinking, striking upon who might be able to help us."

Thanking the friendly soul for answering their questions, they make their way back to the Elder's house, firm in their decision to leave Veran tomorrow to travel to Delmar, whereto Janderas suggested to go earlier.

"Did I not tell you that your sister, my wife, could help us."

"You did, but she is not the only one."

"Hervjol, Ginhal, whoever. I told you."

"You did."

TOGETHER AGAIN: To be in Unelas' house among friends is a blessing to Artias as much as to Janderas; for all that happened, they treasure these moments of fellowship.

Checking on his garment placed by the fireside to dry, Artias feels as if he must announce his joy, saying that he is thankful to have such loyal fellows and praises their names and sacrifices, saying then to Unelas, "Of course, you are among them, Elder."

"Thank you."

"You are welcome."

Laughing Gordes heads for the kitchen, straight fetching a bottle of wine. Telling all of his friends to sit around the table and join in a drink, he grabs a chair and claps his hand upon the tabletop. "Come around, my friends, come around."

"This is not your home!" says Artias. "It is not your home, my friend, nor is that your wine!"

"Unelas said I shall feel at home."

"I have indeed," the Elder states and assures the hunter that he is not bothered about Gordes' behavior in any way.

"See, Artias, as honorable as you are, you might wish to celebrate with me, for I am in love."

"I go lie down," mumbles Arianna and turns in.

"You must be very tiresome," Janderas says to Gordes upon joining him at the table.

"I do my best to get her attention, but it sometimes seems to be as if I am disturbing her in someway."

"Women," Artias explains, "women are a mystery but a delightful one," and he then sits down and lays his hand on Gordes' arm and lets him know (that) "Some day might be the day she will see what a fine man you are."

"I say, Artias," Unelas utters, "why do you look for that fellow Surjes?"

"The knife, as trifle as it may be, could give me an answer to open questions. If the man it belongs to can be found, that is."

"Open questions?" wonders Unelas. "What are you talking about here?"

"Events that haunt me, Unelas—dreadful incidences that leave me without rest."

"What events in particular?"

"I do wish to speak about that; we shall enjoy being together now."

"You sound as if you wish not to speak about these events with me, although you have with my daughter! You shall not keep me in the—"

"She told you—"

"Yes, Artias, she has told me everything."

"Then you know what—"

"Haunts you? Yes, I do, but I advise you to forget Odas. It is for the best that you do, hunter!"

"Why is that?" Janderas utters, staring fiercely at the Elder.

"Because, because I, I—"

"Speak already!"

"I cannot bear the thought of knowing what my daughter had been through there—it makes feel guilty."

Hearing his daughter's tread, he casts a glance back, seeing her approaching him.

"I thought you wish to rest?" he asks her.

"It mustn't," says Arianna, "it mustn't."

"What are you speak of, my daughter?"

"Your ordeal, father. You mustn't feel guilty, not ever shall you feel guilty"—glaring at Artias, she shakes her head at his questions—"for this hunter shall make me remember neither my nor your ordeal any longer!" And she even asks Gordes to speak to Artias so that she can live without being remembered of the horrors of her live. "I cannot bear it anymore."

Holding the bottle of wine aloft in a toast to Artias, Gordes praises the hunter for his endurance. "Your endeavors have no bound; but, please, allow her to forget!"

"I believe it is 'know no bounds'," Janderas interrupts and lays a hand on Artias' arm, saying as honest as a man can be, "but yes, he is right, you are truly one stubborn mule—which is good!"

Gnashing her teeth, Arianna seeks the bedroom, shouting back at everyone but her father, "A blind treader is not going to see what he walks into!"

Rising at once, Artias lays a hand on his heart, wishing to apologize for having dredged up painful memories.

"Please, do please hear me, Arianna, I did not mean to—"

"To what? Intrude into others' lives!" Straight drawing to him, all set to whack him, she cries out, "I wish to forget, only forget; but you do not allow me to!"

"I only—"

"I hate you!" she says, withdrawing into the bedroom, banging close the door.

Confused about her behavior, Artias draws a breath, asking Unelas if he feels the same as his daughter.

"Our actions have consequences, Artias, consequences you may not see, and yet they are there, affecting others as much as yourself; and you certainly do not let anything come in your way—I say this once, do not trouble her."

"But I was not going to speak about Odas—"

"You should let her find her peace," says Gordes; "I have disturbed her enough already. You mustn't, too."

"You are disturbing her?" Janderas asks Gordes, looking on Arianna's behavior as by far more disturbing than Gordes' ever could be.

"All day I have tried to declare my love to her, but she would not hear of it. I say, she needs time for herself."

"Gordes," utters Janderas, eager to give him an advice on how to act. "Let me give you an advice: You must not tell her how much you like her to show her that you do."

"Meaning what?"

"Get her flowers," Artias strikes in. "I mean, if she is such a lovely flower as you say, then you may wish to ask Alarion to join him when he gets flowers for his wife. You could bring her one or two, but say no word when you hand them to her. Simply give them to her, and you will see that she will ask you why; and then, when she does, do not dance around her. Obviously, she does not quite like that. Well, be that as it may, I wish to show you the knife now."

On the table he places the knife, pointing at the engraved name. "There's the name. Now, does any one of you recognizes this blade?"

"What is going on with you, Artias?" asks Unelas. "Have you not come to realize that you—"

"For this matter to be dealt with, I have to inquire, and you even allowed me to. May I proceed now?"

"As you said, it has to be dealt with. Pray proceed."

"Thank you. Now, has any one of you recognized this knife already?"

"I did not," says Janderas.

"Yes, I know—we found it together, my fellow."

The knife, not a beautiful one at all, has two distinctive features: a large cross guard and a pointed, double-edged blade.

"This is no knife, Artias." Gordes draws his knife from a sheath on his boot and lays it on the table. "This is a knife, that a dagger."

"Of course, yes," Janderas mutters, "the cross guard, the blade. Well, hunters do not need a cross guard, so this dagger must belong to someone who—"

"It could belong to Surjes," Artias gives voice to his thoughts, letting his fellows wonder what he means. "The name seems engraved rather unskilled. This weapon, it might have been used to slay someone's family or friends, someone who then took this dagger and carved the name of the man who had slain his nearest and dearest on the blade—who's to say."

"Yes, who's to say," Unelas agrees forthwith.

"With luck we will find out whose it is in Delmar," says Janderas as he gets up to gather his clothes.

He asks Unelas whether he and Artias can stay in his house 'til the rain eases and smiles as he told "most certainly".

Knaves
Of the wildest

Unlike the habitat of the great, mostly terrifying critters living in forests, the environment of those found upon the mountains is harsh and prey often scarce. These creatures, although rather small, can still threaten a grown man and do not shy from preying upon anything bigger than them after longer periods of hungering. Bandits, all of which dwell in caves on mountains, are aware of this and take on long journeys to pass the timberline after hunting in plains or forests. Having no horses (for these animals struggle with icy ground), their journeys are laborious, especially when bearing their kill.

For those currently ascending, the way ahead is long and exerting, and carrying their prey home through deep snow draws on their vitality.

Steeply climbing tracks and rough, narrow paths along vast cliffs dominate their way home. Because their commonly used routes (chosen for fear of and encounter with varmints) are far off those used by others than bandits, they need long to come within sight of their dwelling.

Not far from the cave Gordes tried to reach before falling, they halt and announce their coming with a shout and then wait in the cold for somebody to emerge from beyond.

"What takes them so long!" says the biggest man of the group and inspects the snow-covered ground. Unluckily, the snow that has fallen until now covered all other footprints apart from theirs, making it virtually impossible for him to see whether beasts were here.

"Maybe they did not hear us," his fellows guess, looking at him, though he—a man of vile deeds, walking mantled in boar hides, with a dead body upon his shoulder and a fine sword in his grasp—remains silent for a while, thinking about what could have happened to his kin before making a decision.

"Tendjan," his fellows call him, struggling to carry their prey much longer. "It could be that they did not hear our shout, for the wind, it is blowing, blowing away our voices!"

Yet Tendjan says, "Put down your kill and draw your blades," and he lets the body fall; and with his sword raised, its tip set to pierce whatever there come, he approaches the cave's mouth.

He is the first to enter their dwelling and the first to find the few remaining bones of his kin, among which he finds a skull that was punctured by an arrow and another that was cleaved by a sword. Abundant bite marks on the skulls tell him that critters sought this cave, yet not to hunt but merely to feast upon scenting the dead.

He may be a vile man, acting savagely and wild, killing for joy or gold; but despite all, he is out of flesh and blood, able to cry and feel pain, and he sheds a tear on realizing that his kin have been taken from him.

In rage he flings his blade upon the rocky ground, crying at his fellows to search the cave for survivors; and he tells them to be quick, for they must leave again soon to hunt.

"And avenge!" say his fellows. "We will find whomever done this, and with blades and arrows we will fall upon 'em, and we shall hang 'em and cut 'em and burn the lots of 'em!"

"He will know whom it was!" says Tendjan, glaring into the empty.

"How could he!" utters a man with long hair and a short beard. Holding a bow ready to use but keeping his sword sheathed, he utters angrily, "He could not know—he asked us to deal with the people and said we shall return home afterwards. If anything he knew, he would have told us, would have sent someone to us days ago!"

"All but those we claimed our own have been dealt with already, alongside of Tarion. Why would he tell me to do that if he hand't had a reason? Why would he tell me to kill them all, all of his fare? Odd, strange, I say. But Tarion, before I threw him down, he spoke of a hunter, told me: 'It is all to be blamed on the hunter, a man whose kin slay yours.'"

"So what do you think of doing now, Tendjan?"

"We eat, rest, and prepare to leave at sunrise. I must see Unelas! It is about time this play ends!"

Seeking understanding
Many miles they traveled to find out more about the name on the blade, but even if they were to discover more, they would not awake to the sinister doings of the weapon's owner.

Seemingly endless rainfall drenches the earth, creating deep rills in the soil. Although the cloudburst had stopped, it returned not long after Artias and Janderas left Veran. On their way to Delmar, the rain never stops pouring down the skies; and creeks grow to tearing rivers, and lakes overflow; and the clouds gather, come together to a great cover that darkens the earth.

Wet and freezing Janderas sits on his horse, complaining silently about their misfortune.

"Rain, rain, nothing but rain," he grunts, hoping that the warm light of the Sun will touch his skin again soon; and, indeed, the weather clears within a day: the dark clouds fade and the Sun breaches through the gloom, casting light and warmth upon wetted earth.

Ever so often, when they grant their horses a pause, they see birds rising and deer grazing; and they witness the great creatures of the Sun (Arjovan) roaming the land, many of which come forth fierce but soon strike them as harmless, for the green is all they are keen on; and there shows the eastern mountain before them, so endlessly high and mighty in appearance that they simply stare at this monumental art of nature for some time. Nearby this one great mountain (Camveral as it will be named in the years to come), the other one strikes them as small but enormous it is even so. The massif is seen behind them, the highest mountain of which soars over the land beneath.

At a truly larger prairie they draw to a halt and pause—as they have at every glade they passed.

"Soon we will reach the plain," says Janderas and untethers the horses to let them graze freely. "Let us not pause for too long." He then, without words, steps away from his fellow and gazes into the distance.

"I never though I would take such delight in traveling on horseback," utters Artias joyfully.

Janderas does not answer. Staring south absorbed in thought, he remains in silence.

After a while Artias steps to him, looking in the same direction as his fellow. There before them, beyond the prairie, he sees the largest and tallest mountain ever to stand on land, rising in a foreign realm.

"Are you looking at the Ranmostau?" he asks.

"There is a structure in this prairie, Artias. Have you ever wandered this grassland before?"

"Yes, with Gordes and Hentario, but we did not go—"

"Even from the distance, I can feel the peril in the air."

"I don't understand."

"That being you believe to be divine, I know it is connected to that place somehow. In what way, I do not know. I wished to find out; but, sadly, my efforts were in vain."

"What lies there far off our sight?"

"I think that being is not alone—I believe there are more, many more."

"Janderas, what are you talking about exactly?"

"It is not made my Man. No. Black walls, vast towers, and you can hear roars from there—unearthly cries, Artias. There were times when I heard them at night as often as at day."

"I do not see anything."

"We are too far away. I stood on the canyon, trying to evade the tearing water that flooded it." Nodding at the river running through this grassland, he says, "I know that you should not travel near this mountain (Camveral) when rain is falling; there are too many rockslides then. But I did not know of the falls the mountain brings forth when ice and snow begins to melt. I was on the canyon, hearing the falls rumble, witnessing the mass of water flooding the canyon and this entire prairie 'til the earth took in the water, leaving behind a river 'til autumn. Yes.

I say, if you ascend the canyon walls and stand upon, looking over this area, you will be able to see a massive wall surrounding an array of towers. Do not be a fool and mistaken it for a city like I did. The closer you go, the clearer it becomes that it is unlike any other structure on earth. There is no gate, and yet you can see a wall, a bulwark; and I tell you, Artias, I tell you, I could hear the sound of the fray, and I could hear roars and growls. I shuddered and ran off, deeming it to be a dragon's cage."

"Dragons do not exists."

"I know. But the only other explanation is that this land, Arjovan, was never ours to claim—a worrisome, even dreadful thought."

"If this land was not free, then there would have been roads, villages, people, signposts, cities, but there weren't—all we found was nature!"

"If you would have entered from the south, you would have thought differently. I had seen quite a few tribes who told me not to go there. 'It is not unruled,' they said. 'And beware, there be dragons.' I do not believe in mythical creatures. All I know is that there live things in Arjovan we better be aware of. I tell you this as a friend. And, Artias, do not talk about this with anyone. Neither I nor you, nor anyone else, shall go to that place. As I see it, people haven't had any problems so far—we best keep it this way."

"But—"

"If ever you say something, people could feel drawn there—to those grounds of ash—to find out what it is lest they lose the land. It mustn't come that far."

"I shall not speak to anyone about this, my friend. Yet, my fellow, why did you want to find out about that place if you say that such actions could let us lose our grounds, or maybe even our lives."

"Do not think me a fool, Artias. If I had found that being, I would not have followed it anywhere near that place. I merely wished to find out more about it without risking anything."

"I spoke to me, Janderas. In a tongue I could not understand it spoke to me, although it did understand my words, of that I am sure."

"You have once told me so. I couldn't really believe you, though. This is not the time to discuss that anyway. I just wanted to warn you. Let us move on now, Artias."

Nodding Artias hitches the seven horse to the leading one again, the stallion. Then he mounts the mare and waits for Janderas to be in the saddle.

They carry on at midday and ride along the border of the eastern forest to the northern plain, for days thinking about all the myths and tales told by seamen alike warriors; and they wonder how many of these stories could be based upon truth. The mere thought of all that is yet to be discovered strikes them with fear: somethings are best to remain but folk tale. They ease their worries nevertheless, for upon espying Delmar after days of traveling through ancient lands, is much to their relief.

Once they stand before the gate, looking up at the guards in the towers, they smile and ask to be allowed in.

"Of course," say the guards, letting them enter forthwith.

Through the gate they enter into known grounds and are straight greeted by men whose only duty is to take care of the horses' needs. Handing over the rein of the leading horse after a short exchange, Janderas says "Each of these brave animals shall be given care and fare, and do groom them thoroughly."

Watching how the horses are being escorted to the stable, he draws a breath, praising these fair animals for their endurance.

"They are truly fine creatures," says Ginhal, approaching Janderas. He and Hervjol are the first who embrace him and Artias, saying that they are glad to see them and asking them both to join in a drink with them.

"If only I had time," says Artias.

Tanara joins the group then, hugging her beloved spouse as warmly as her brother, with a smile telling them both how glad she is to see them here; and she says to Janderas, "I hope I am not going to see you part again!"

When Hjos emerges walking to them, saying while drawing nearer, "You should stay for longer than a mere day this time, Artias," Tanara can tell by her brother's look that this will not be so.

"What is going on?" she asks him.

"There is an urgent matter to discuss," says Artias, glimpsing at everyone he attracts.

"What about?" inquires Hjos, standing before the hunter, who is ringed by his kin. Looking at Janderas, who is of his closets friends, he wonders aloud, "What is so important that we are not even greeted."

"You will be told," says Janderas and pats Artias on the shoulder, telling him where he best gather his kin.

"The tavern," he says, "there we shall come together."

Stepping forth, out of the crowd, Artias turns to face his kin and asks them to follow him.

"For reasons that allow no delay, you must assemble in the tavern at once," he explains.

"You did not even greet us the first time," one of his kin says, treading quickly towards him. "Now, now you suddenly return and tell us to gather."

"I understand your resent. It is not that I wish to make you feel bitter, thought this matter I am dealing with grants me no pause—please, follow me."

And everyone follows him to the tavern, whereas those who do not know of the meeting are send for. Until everyone is present, Artias waits in silence, roaming his eyes over the fine wood out of which this tavern came to be, and he looks at the images of trees engraved on the wood and at the fire burning in the chimney beside him; and then, when finally all of his kindred are in the tavern, he looks at them and lays the dagger on a table, asking everyone to come around and have a look.

"Surjes is carved on the blade. Does any one of you know who that is, or perhaps the dagger seems familiar to you?"

But Hervjol withdraws from the table and demands that everyone leave, apart from those directly involved.

"Be on your way home now," he says, stating then that this meeting is over.

"It has yet began!" utters Artias.

"Have patience."

With annoyance the people leave the tavern, struggling greatly to cope with Hervjol's suddenly rough persona; they wish to know what is going on. No matter how great everyone's frustration may be, Hervjol, Elder of Delmar, has his reasons for keeping them in the dark. He nevertheless declares that they be told by Ginhal, who may stay together with Janderas, what was discussed behind closed doors.

"Sit down, Artias," he says upon seeing the last one leave. "Ginhal, Janderas, join us at the table."

Hervjol takes the dagger and looks at it, saying that he never thought to hear the name it tells again.

"Surjes is no man you want to know anything about, Artias. Of all the fellows in this land, he is the last you wish to know of. His actions were—"

"*Beheaded be my foe and dreaded my name**," Janderas utters angrily. "Where can he be found?"

"Be still and listen. Surjes crept about the forests, preying on those who had come to this land. He believed that every life he slay will grant him a hundred years to his own. Driven by his madness to be immortal one day, he fell upon many men and women, showing mercy only to children, for they were not old enough to give him these hundred years he desired."

"From where do you know this?" asks Janderas. "Did he come upon you?"

"He was my friend. I did not know of his doings until I set about finding who's responsible for the killing of all the poor souls who had gone missing. I found him in the forest, lurking in the bushes like a beast. It was there where I killed him."

"If he is dead as you say," says Artias, "then what about this dagger?"

"You must know that many of the children who had lost their parents to Surjes' strive for immortality grew to men and women deprived of guidance. They became foul in heart, forming tribes of their own, bandit tribes. It is very well possible that Surjes is thought to be alive and hunted by these tribes, which is why I ask you to stay out of this, Artias. Let them search to allow the people of this land—those who are true and honorable in heart—not fear a bandit attack."

"But the dagger, Hervjol, the dagger we found in a pond not far from where people had been assailed by beasts of prey—"

Artias hushes as a thought crosses his mind, and after no longer than instant, he asks Hervjol how likely it is that some of the children who had lost their parents were forced to feed on anything they could find to survive.

"What exactly are you asking me, Artias?"

"Can it be that they ate flesh."

"Well, as you might know, some bandits eat their dead fellows as they are of the belief that no fare shall go to waste."

"I have slain many bandits but did not know they are corpse-eaters." Janderas thumps the table with his fist, shouting out his abhorrence, "This land, it is as if it be cursing every soul walking its ground."

"Are you sure Surjes is dead?" Artias inquires of Hervjol.

"His head I cut off, Artias. There is no way he is alive!"

"Does he have relatives?"

"We all have, Artias, but whether they are alive, that I do not know."

"But—"

"ENOUGH," cries Janderas. "Artias, stop acting so stubborn! If you want to know, then ask Arianna, and if she does not speak, find a way to make her divulge to you that mystery that is dominating your every thought."

"Listen, Janderas, if Surjes is dead, then why did Tarion and Ardegan speaking of him?"

"That is what Arianna told you, and it must not be true. That woman is strange anyway, Artias—I cannot but feel uncomfortable around her!"

Confused, Hervjol looks from one to the other and eventually asks what they talk about and why the dagger is of such importance to Artias, who thereupon tells him about all that had taken place, with very word robbing his kin's breath.

"Horrible," is all that Hervjol says, looking upon some of the people of Odas as savage beasts. He had never heard of anything alike: that a village had been raised only to keep people at a place for an utterly cruel reason shocks him to his very bones, and he says that if the foul beings of that place ... not be dead, he would kill them himself. Be that as it may, he wonders why they buried Arianna's boy and Ardegan whereas they could have eaten them.

"That is obvious," says Janderas. "They did that because they could not have Artias nor the others see their doings. Tarion, he said that Artias should not have stayed in Arianna's house, so why would they eat flesh while he is still there—they couldn't."

"But everyone was brought away, Janderas!" Artias utters.

"Because of the beast!"

"No, no. As I said, your emergence hindered Tarion from carrying out his plan. I tell you, Janderas, he was about to met with someone as you came. And whoever that was, this dagger was his; and I will—I say, I shall—find this person."

Hervjol rises from his chair, glancing at the dagger.

"How old was Tarion?" he asks.

"Very old. He did not seem as if he had much time left."

"He could have certainly encountered Surjes once, although since I had killed him many years have gone by. I ask myself, what if he and the other fellow—ah, what was his name? Ardegan?"

"Ardegan, yes."

"What if they spoke of the owner of the dagger and not of the man to be slain."

"This is pointless," utters Janderas. "We'll never know who it belongs to. I say, ask Arianna."

"I certainly would," says Hervjol.

The Face behind the Mask
When the fiend's doings unraveled, his foul associates came forth and his vile kin showed ... face, acting beyond even their leader's wickedness; and then their prey struck upon who's coming can set them free.

Once more Artias and Janderas journey to Veran after no more than a night's rest in Delmar, much to everyones' disappointment, especially as days will go by 'til either of them will be seen again.

Until now, Janderas feels sorry for his spouse, with whom he supposed to spend most of his days.

"She asked me to stay, Artias. 'Please, stay,' she said; 'you shall not leave me alone again.' I love her, with all my heart I do; but she makes me feel caged."

"I do not see where that would be the case, Janderas. If anything she wishes than to have you near."

"When I left in search of the being, she was angry at me; and when she found out that I had joined in the hunt for those bandit tribes upon the mountain, she was angry at me. I mostly do not say anything when I leave, because I do not know how long I will be away—"

"So you just leave her in the dark?"

"Yes, well, sometimes."

"That is not good. You should share your every thought with her and never take her love for granted."

"It is not easy to always say what troubles you when you try, truly try as best as you can, to be strong—not for yourself but for her."

"To me, that sounds like an excuse!"

"An excuse for what? No, Artias, I am an honest man."

"To others you are, but not to yourself. I think you struggle with showing your feelings, because you think she could look upon you as a coward."

"What—how dare you say that to me!"

"I try to help you, my fellow."

"Then why do you speak in her favor."

"I merely give you a disinterested opinion."

"No, you do not!"

"I speak from a neutral perspective, Janderas; and I say you are burdened by the past, forced into caging yourself by thinking of what you should have done to help fight injustice on your way to Arjovan. Hence you keep your feelings to yourself, trying as best as you can to be the man you think she desires…

"Why are you saying such things?"

…what you do not see is that you are the man she decided to be with…

"I do not see where this is going!"

…you and only you she chose, so be fair to her and share your feelings with her before it will be too late!"

"What is that supposed to mean?"

"Each day could be your last, my fellow."

There is truth in Artias' words, a truth Janderas must face for his well being and that of his spouse; however, despite how often he broods over all that which he should have told his dearest already, he grunts shortly and says to his horse, "Be glad you aren't human!"

"Sooner or later," says Artias, "sooner or later you will have to deal with your feelings, my friend."

For the rest of the day Janderas thinks about what he could say to his dear wife. Now that they have no horses in tow, they can travel easier and with less difficulties, giving him the changes to face the truth to find the right words.

Many a time they ride at a gallop, trot or walk on foot by their horses, taking no breather for long: they mustn't pause as often as before, when they had to ward and guide every horse they had with them. Still and all, they need several days to come within sight of Veran.

At sunrise, when people are already up and working on the stockade, they first see the village.

At once they dismount and go on by foot. With heavy steps treading through the mud towards Veran, they see Gordes hewing the top of a trunk to a point, with swears hacking his way through the wood alongside of Alarion.

Upon seeing his fellows, Gordes lets the axe fall and greets them warmly before uttering loudly, "I say, making these stakes is hard work."

"I guess you have to get used to the weight of that axe," says Janderas.

"No, not really. The weight, it does not bother me. But, anyway, what brought you here?"

"Horses, apparently—all the way."

"No, I mean, why—"

"He was joking, Gordes," says Artias. "Say, where is Arianna?"

"I think she is in the tavern. She said she would like to do something, so Unelas said she can help the barman—not that I forgot his silence."

"His silence?" wonder Janderas.

"Yes, he seems to be a silent man. Artias knows what I mean."

Looking at the hunter, Gordes tells him that "the fellow apologized for saying nothing". "As if that is going to change anything. Remember, we had to break in Unelas' house to find—"

"Gordes," says Artias, "I really need to talk to Arianna."

"Are you saying you came here because of her only?"

"It is important, my fellow—I will gladly explain everything to you later."

Quickly they leave their friend, promising him to return again once the reason for their visit has been dealt with. They quicken their pace in sight of the tavern and enter in a rush, wasting not a moment when they see Arianna sweeping the floor.

"I need to talk to you," Artias says at once.

Shocked into silence she gawks at him, shaking her head slightly.

"Why are you looking at him like that," Janderas utters fiercely. "You do good to answer his questions, or else I—"

"Enough!" Artias insists that he not threaten her, saying, "Not you nor I shall act foul," and he then looks in Arianna's eyes to see whether she avoids his gaze when he says, "I will not leave until you have spoken to me."

"You come and go, come and go—why?"

"Because questions need to be answered."

She can only wonder why, oh, why is this man so fervently searching for answers. "Why, for all, are you pestering me so often?"

"Sit down," demands Janderas, "sit down now and answer!"

Having no other choice, she can't but agree and takes a seat at a table, asking Artias to sit down as well and if possible "send that savage man away."

But Artias asks right away why, "Why did you and the others leave Odas?"

To hear this disturbs her utterly, and she raises her voice and shouts at him to finally leave her alone with these questions.

"Answer!" Janderas commands. "It is making him sick not to know. Besides, you do not seem to be very trustworthy. You are avoiding the question, I can see!"

"No."

"Then speak."

"It was our decision. Mine and the others'."

"Not Tarion's?" asks Artias.

"No, he wanted us to stay, tried to convince everyone to stay over and over again, but nobody would listen to him, and so he had made the letter and he had us sign it because, at last, we did leave because of the—"

Sudden clamor cast a hush over everyone. All but known voices are shouting about; and screams, wails, and begs follow the bellowing of men; and women are heard crying and children squalling—and Artias rises from his chair, at once glancing at his companion.

"What is going on out there!" Janderas utters and hurries to the front door, straight dashing out along of Artias, closely followed by Arianna.

And there they witness men of foul deeds forcing every soul of this village out of their houses, impelling them to join those who have already been wreathed by their comrades; and others—all the same vile as their kindred—are keeping Gordes and the brave he is among at bay with spears and bows. Side by side with every guard of Veran, they drive the people closer together, savagely dragging the last few to the rest while declaring to slay whomever may rebel.

"What is the meaning of this?" cries Janderas.

From the midst of the wicked comes forth a man with a body dressed in fell, who sneers as he sees Unelas emerging from his house and laughs as Gordes cries, "Cowards!"

Forthwith Arianna leaves Artias' side (thrusting Janderas away from her as he tries to seize her arm) and swiftly walks over to the man, saying that she is ever so glad to see him.

"I cannot bear that man any longer!" says she, glaring at Gordes. "He is always dancing around me — I say, do kill him now!"

"What game are you playing!" Artias, though often a calm man, can barely keep his fury at bay. All the wicked souls around, no matter whether they are under arms, cannot frighten him; and "Should any harm come to the people, I shall slay you all!"

"What a fool you are," Unelas utters, raising his head in triumph.

"Answer me, what game are you playing!"

End of the game, ceasing her play, Arianna unveils the beast within her and steps forth, overwhelmed by an urge to let Artias see her true face.

"I sunk to my knees crying and all mine you were. It was so easy, so easy, Artias. Dealing with you has never been much of a challenge. It had more of a play than a challenge. Yes, a cat toying with its prey — that is all it was. But you became a problem nevertheless, an annoying, constantly pestering and pressing problem. Tell me, why did you want to stay in my house? My house where you had no right to be! The beast should have eaten you. It was so easy, all he had to do is lure you to its jaws; but, no, that did not go as it should have."

"You misleading witch!"

"Witch? Oh, no, I am no witch, Artias. You think I am wicked, but let us not forget who killed Beras and how. 'You are the wicked soul here,' wasn't that what you said? You know, I must say, that you killed him was quite impressing. How did it feel to let loose your inner beast? It felt good, didn't it?"

"Oh, what I will do to you when I get my hands on—"

"Say, did you like what lies beneath my house?"

"I see you are a corpse-eater like them—"

"Like whom? Tarion, Beras, and the othe—"

"HUSH! YOU LIED ABOUT EVERYTHING! YOU, YOU ARE AMONG THEM, AND SO YOU SHALL DIE WITH THEM!"

"No, that is not true. I did not lie about everything; all that I told you about my boy was true, and all that had happened to him was also true. I merely did not say that I had killed his mother. Her skin was so soft, so soft and tender that I could not resist to taste. Guilt, though, guilt made me care for the poor kid I had terrified so terribly."

Her every word is a mockery; and she takes, above all else, pride in her deeds, considering all but her own beneath her.

"Do not speak of guilt," shouts Artias. "'Only until he grow old enough.' Do you remember who said that? It wasn't any one of the others, not Tarion nor Beras nor Gilgaron. No!"

"But, Artias, how can you say something like that? He tried to run away so very often that I felt as if I were a bad mother, although I told him how quick death can be. 'Do not try to run,' I said, 'or you will die.' He would not listen to me

—stubborn little brat. The last time he had tried to leave me, he ran right into the beast, as I say, death can be quick—"

"You are disgusting me!" Artias quivers with rage, yearns to avenge all who had suffered by her and her kind's doings.

"I will cut your head straight off your neck," cries Janderas and draws his swords, immediately finding himself in the aim of the bowmen.

"Release your arrows," he yells at them, "release them now and I will set upon you! Do not miss, for all you have is one shot!"

"Hush!" cries Arianna, "or I'll have every child brought down!

And now to you, Artias—you, the brave hunter, the blind treader—, let me ask you, do you have any idea what was actually going on? My father, do you assume he built a stockade because of your advice, your warnings? Hah, how naive. Be the fool that you are to the end of your days. 'Oh, Arianna, why did you leave, why return,' why this and that, and on and on and on you go. It is very simple, very simple indeed, but you never—"

"What does it matter now! Whatever be, you will die here—I promise you this!"

"WATCH YOUR MOUTH, ARTIAS! I AM NOT WHOM YOU THINK I AM!"

Gordes cannot believe what he hears. The woman who saved his life turns out to be one of the wickedest fiends in this land.

"I wanted to marry you," he says, "but now I see through you."

"Be quiet! You know why I saved you? I tell you why: decaying meat is disgusting to eat. Now, you and all the others go into the tavern, and there you stay until we come to get you!"

"GET MOVING," Unelas demands, casting a shiver down Artias' spine.

"You!" Artias utters with disgust. "I trusted you!"

"You ask too many questions. Just because you find my dagger doesn't mean you have to trouble me with questions. And before you ask, no, I am not Surjes, but he slew my parents. People like him, people who are driven by their strive like you are to blame for our misery. I will teach you to fear me, Artias. You will tremble at my name like Tarion did."

"HE WAS LIKE YOU, AND YOU WILL DIE LIKE HIM!"

"Ah, I see, you have delusions again. Tarion could never face me. I tell you, Artias, not once he dared to stand before me. He rather live in Odas, where the beast you ought to bring down took our precious supplies from us...

"Dare you call people supplies!"

...he could not deal with the thought of seeing me only because I once, just once, broke his knee...

"I will kill you, Unelas."

...you know what came then, what he forced me to do because of his fear of me? Shall I tell you? I'll gladly do...

"HUSH YOUR MOUTH!"

...I told my fellow Tendjan to kill everyone in the feasting chamber and let Tarion there. Arianna's house lies in the forest, so how long do you think it took 'til the first critter came?"

"I slew him!" Janderas shouts. "And you I will too."

"So then he managed to get out of the hole. Should I care? No. Dead is dead. And you, Artias, you—"

221

"Silence! Or I shall—"

"Or you shall what? Behead me. Oh, no, Artias, I want you to see what you have brought about: a stockade allowing all the people we have to be kept within, without a way to run or escape. You must understand that you force me to make you continue building your own prison—it cannot be left incomplete."

"Come to me and say that again, just a little closer now."

Smiling Unelas tells his daughter to let the archers aim at children and women before he approaches Artias, saying: "Stab me down and you can see how easily and arrow pierces a child's skull. No masquerade anymore, see who I am, Artias, and look at me when I say: The people of Odas should have been brought here as soon as the stockade is standing. Unfortunately, you forced my daughter to haste. Look around, Artias, look and see what you have caused. Not to mention that your friend there (Janderas) has crossed our plans just as well. Or, no, I should say, he saved my daughter from beasts, allowing her to mislead you even more. Even so, he is a problem. Oh, and before I forget, that dagger you bear, hand it to me. I gave it to my daughter, and she is the only one to own it."

"I recognize those leather strings," Artias shouts at Tendjan. "Alike the ones your fellows on the mountain had. You want me to tell you how I cut them down, how my blade drove through their guts!"

"You will pay for their deaths," Tendjan vows. "I am here just for you, all the way I took just for you; and I say, Unelas, let him built the stockade with his kind 'til their legs bend and they fall to their knees before me. There, that man beside him and Gordes shall join him. Three man, one stake in half a day, or three people lose their lives—yes, Artias, I will make your life a painful strive for death."

"I know now why you did not care about the voices Alarion had heard!" Gordes says to Unelas, and then continues to Arianna's ally: "And you, you I will slay for what has been done to my frien—" Forthwith an arrow hits his chest, lancing through his skin into the flesh, puncturing a lung. Within sight of his fellows he falls on the ground, his blood gurgling in his throat.

"GORDES!" his friend's cry, yet they are not allowed to take but a pace towards him.

"One step," says Unelas, "and you see the children and women fall."

Gordes' last breath, drawn in sight of the woman he loved, a woman who regards his death with joy.

Janderas gnashes his teeth, pledging to carve her name upon his blade and drive it through her body 'til her heart falls out of her chest, "down into the dirt".

Looking at the hunter, Arianna asks whether he desires to have her name on a blade, too; yet Artias says nothing, nothing at all; the thought of what he could have averted if only he had seen the evil that nestled in the heart of a father and his daughter is killing him.

While the people are forced to herd into the tavern, Unelas enjoys the power he holds. He has claimed everyone's life his to use and command and with satisfaction observes the archers surrounding the tavern, and he looks at his guards as they close the door, with a nod signing him that everyone is within.

"Do not let your eyes off them!" says he. "Two of you must watch them, or else they may get ideas. And, listen here, make sure they hush; I do not want to hear them clamoring—no, wails, no squalls, make them hush by force if need be."

Two guards enter the tavern thereupon, shouting their prey into silence.

Just to know that Artias blames himself for not seeing through to this game pleases Unelas tremendously; and he then returns his dagger to Arianna and says to Artias, "You are a hunter but as blind as none before you!"

"You will die, Unelas. This is a promise!"

"I will show you what I can do to the people should you try to take up arms." At once signing the guards to take every horse to the stable, he continues: "You and your fellow raise this stockade now—you shall labor to the day you fall to your knees."

HARDSHIP: Toiling away all day long, given neither food nor time to rest, Janderas can hardly raise the axe much longer at dusk and Artias struggles with digging the holes for the many stakes they are to raise on their own.

As soon as the guards talk to each other, watching him less closely, Artias lets the shovel fall and heads to his fellow, saying to whomever commands that he return to work, "We must ready the stake to raise it."

With revulsion, overwhelming fury and resent, he treads past the guards to Janderas.

"Listen," he demands in a whisper, "our kin, they do not know what is gong on here. We are on our own. Howeve—"

Upon seeing the guards looking at him, he says that he is searching for an axe, though they say, "You better be doing just that," and approach him at once.

"We have only one axe," says Artias; "You took the others, leaving us with almost nothing."

"If you know you have but one, then why do you search for another? What are you trying here!"

"We must get this stake ready," utters Janderas. "We must prepare it to raise it!"

Drawing a sword, one guard steps closer to Artias, then and there striking him with the pommel.

"Damn you!" cries Janderas, trying to catch his fellow's fall.

"Hold your tongue or you will lose it!" Glaring at Artias, whose mouth is wreathed in blood, the guard says that he shall use the shovel for an axe.

"How shall I—"

"Get your shovel now, or else!"

Nodding Artias complies, swaying as he rises from the ground.

Having fetched the shovel, he sets about using it like an axe, feeling his anger growing at the guards' laughter. They mock him, saying that he really took the shovel for an axe. Eventually, though, they join their comrades again.

"I should cleave his skull with a shovel," says Janderas. "Say, are you badly hurt?"

"No. Liste—"

"I thought they ward the people; but, no, they are bandits and corpse-eaters and foul and rotten, and damn they be for betraying those in their care...

"Janderas!"

...you said you were banished? Yes, of course you were. Probably the easiest way to deal with you without making the people suspicious was by sending you out into the wilds where you will be preyed on an—"

"Shut your damn mouth and listen before the guards see me talking to you again!"

"Speak then, before I lose myself. I begin to think about a headlong attack, so you better be quick with your words."

"The archers are watching the tavern. I should be able to dash into the forest. They will not follow me—"

"You cannot make it to Delmar in time, Artias—not on foot!"

"All I need to do is call out to every beast near and far to come to me. Do what you must to reach the tavern when you see me returning. Barricade the door and do not leave!"

"Are you mad? You will die, you fool!"

"Trust me."

"If you die I am going to kill you myself!"

Smiling Artias turns to leave, glimpsing at the guards before taking to his heels.

The guards take note of his escape rather quickly and forthwith come together to a group to pursue him. Many of them are quick on their feet and gain ground on him quickly. Fortunately, Artias has, above all else, excellent endurance. And he runs, he runs without end until embraced by trees and then halts in his tracks and looks back, seeing his foes ceasing their pursuit.

The sky is darkening rapidly, letting him see virtually nothing in the forest; and soon he will be engulfed in utter darkness; and the guards are aware of this, even call after him, "Let the night cage you and the beasts have you," and they also say, "Die in the knowing that your friend will be slain now!"

Allies

Beasts of prey: They are found creeping around the forest, roaming the plains, walking the mountains, hunting to feed their offspring; and when they wake at the onset of night, their cries make known the great (man-eaters) they are among. And these he set about finding.

Unarmed and alone, at the onset of night trudging through the realm of beast, Artias' life hinges upon good fortune. From all the beasts he fears, those among the earliest of critters terrify him to his very core; and these carnivores roused just a moment ago and are now on the prowl, lurking for prey. They can be heard, their presence felt as the touch of wind upon skin; and in the luster of the moon or the sphere of torchlight, their eyes appear as shining orbs in the dark.

And there are many that prey on large animals as often as they do upon men. In their realm, life is quick to end. However deadly, each critter may be regarded as no other than an ally for this one night.

Drawing up his courage, to the very last bit of his courage, Artias screams out into the night, with dread calling every critter, every beast and man-eater near and far to come around for a feast; and he even sinks his teeth into his own arm to let his blood drive their taste for human flesh.

Only able to see the glade behind him, illuminated by the light of the mood shining down upon the grass, he slows down his pace, heading on straight, deeper into the gloom. He is set to prevail, willing to take any risk to prevail. Apart from losing the glade out of sight, there is virtually nothing he would not do to succeed.

Seemingly fearless of death, he raves and shouts and screams, seeing his life resting in the hands of fate; and his actions are destined to a cold embrace, awakening him to the outcome of his efforts, letting him grow aware of the eyes in the dark: he can feel it watching him, somewhere within the darkness waiting for him.

One last time he cries, howling as if he were in unending pain, and then he walks away, all at once beginning to run through the dark towards the light, hoping that he can keep up his pace. Hearing it rushing through the greenery towards him, he tries to run even quicker, endeavorers to outrun death itself.

He aimed at drawing beasts to him, in the end attracting a pack of critters he cannot outrun: even at his quickest pace, he is significantly slower than them. But whereas it seems as if they were pursuing him, they do indeed follow him, for they know that these beings—as he is—only rarely roam alone: should they be led to a herd, large quantities of fare await. As much as Artias knows about beasts; little it is, even so. He would not ever expect that certain critters have the ability to assess an approach and foretell their prey's movement to achieve the best outcome of a hunt. No. Even now, he assumes death to be certain should they catch up. Luckily, the glade is close by; he did not proceed too far off its edge lest he lose orientation and be eaten.

IN VERAN: the guards are about to come down upon Janderas. Gathering together around him after informing Unelas of Artias' escape, they say to him that they have been told to make him pay for his fellow's flight, speaking on with contempt (that) "We shall flog you, and we shall break your arm, and if ever you moan, we shall behead you!"

Frowning at these men before him, Janderas spits at their feet, saying with resolution that he fears no man upon this Earth, "for you are but cases of flesh, blood and bone!"

"Flesh and bone, you say!" Surrounding him at once with drawn blades, they demand that he outstretch an arm. "Do so now, or we cut them off both!"

One of the guards—a formidable opponent versed in fighting—steps forth, holding the tip of his sword under Janderas' chin. Only slightly he raises his foe's head with the blade, saying that no man shall greet his death with head bowed; and he then says, "My blade will go into your flesh and through your bone and beyond; and your head will fall off, and your body will drop into the dirt, and I—"

"You are the dirt I tread on—nothing more!"

Janderas has come to be one of the most fearsome warriors ever since deciding to take up arms against bandit tribes and will not bow before this blackguard nor any of the others, yet the first strike ever to split his lip comes out of nowhere and hits him hard, straight sending him to his knees.

Tendjan emerges from the group with Arianna, looking down on Janderas.

"One clout and you fall down before me," says he, booting his victim to the ground. "And now, now you will cringe at my might!"

ARRIVAL: Artias comes in sight of the glade and dashes through the low-growing vegetation at the forest's edge, keeping up his pace across the glade.

The moon is shining whole, revealing the beasts on his tail: these mighty creatures are among the earliest of critters he fears so greatly, with claws to hold on to their prey and maws to tear off large chunks of flesh. Manes of gray fur mantle most of their necks and the growth of hair beneath their lower jaws displays each creature's position in the hierarchy of the pack by lengths and color. And the prime one, the leading beast with the longest of beards remains behind him at all times, growling and yapping at the others, whereupon they force Artias to run even faster by pretending to lunge at him, at times drawing so close to him that he is even willing to die from exhaustion just to get away; fortunate for him, he is close to Veran by now: if he would not be near, they would not follow him for much longer but set for an attack.

Artias is on the verge, barely able to keep running at this speed: his legs struggle to bear him, and the beasts might fall on him, and when about to lose his breath, he sees the guards in Veran, and they see him and the beasts he is fleeing from.

Straight calling the bowmen to aid them, they withdraw from Janderas and cry at Tendjan to command them, whereas others drop arms and run off.

In sight of the fleeing, some of the beasts leave the pack. Now in pursuit, their actual speed seems without equal; they need but a moment to catch up.

BRAVERY: Janderas can see his fellow trying to outrun the beasts and forthwith charges at one of the guards to claim his foe's blade and take up arms. Striking at the knee with his foot, he forces the guard on the ground and stomps upon his skull, at once taking up the blade and driving it thro' the fiend's chest before he seeks to aid Artias. Heedless of the arrows that are released at the beasts, he strives to assist him.

Despite such a valorous act, which many would acclaim as heroic, Artias is enraged at his fellow's boldness and only able to raise his voice once to cry, "RUN TO THE TAVERN!"

But with the sword held aloft, Janderas runs to his fellow, striking at the beast in the fore. Owing to their numbers, the group of guards and archers ahead attract the pack more than any other prey in reach. Henceforth, Janderas and Artias appear as a trifle claim to the beasts.

And all but one critter fall into Veran, coming upon the guards with claws that cut open their guts and chests, and jaws that crush their skulls, arms and legs. Amid their own the guards strike and fight and desperately try to stay alive. They cry at each other, scream at one another, and howl as they are set upon; and the guards in the tavern bolt out, willing to aid their fellows, calling out to ever one within sight to find shelter in the tavern.

Those who witness the creatures—these great beasts with gnashing teeth and dreadful screeches—tearing and ripping apart their fellows or dragging them away into the dark where only screams make known the taken's fate, are struck by sheer terror. Panic overcomes them, and no more they fight but try to find shelter in the houses—but, it is as Artias always knew, a simple wooden door cannot keep a man-eater from entering, and not ever a pack.

"BEGONE," the guards cry from beyond the door, witnessing its destruction, at all times hearing the growls of the horror that awaits.

And whoever tries to enter the tavern is left to stand before a barred door, soon finding themselves in the jaws of man-eaters, which claws and fangs sink into their flesh; and if not fated to die this way, then they are to feel the force of such a critter's strike, which every claw cuts through skin and flesh, cleaving organs or rupturing them whole.

LOST: Tendjan darts into a house to take shelter with a few of his fellows. Slamming close the door, he straight orders the others to barricade it with anything they find.

"No!" says one of them. "We must run, Tendjan, we must run! You saw what happened to the others—YOU SAW IT!"

"If you run, I shall slay you myself!"

"WE WILL DIE IF WE—"

They fall into silence at the sound of a thud and forth on gape at the front door, with blades held in shaking hands. Then comes the roar from beyond their shelter; and at the beast's charge, the wood embedding the hinges begins to burst. The entire door wavers along with its frame each time the beast runs into it; and the wood splits and begins to crack, giving in to the force.

How quickly the door is being shattering urges Tendjan into taking actions. Charging headlong, he rams the sword through the fractured wood, sure to have injured the beast on hearing its wail.

"STAB IT DOWN!" cry his fellows. "STAB IT DOWN!"

Try as he might, Tendjan cannot repel the beast. It does not cease its assail and keeps raging for entrance, getting wilder each time he attempts to pierce its flesh.

An awkward moment is to follow his next strike: having been pierced again, the beast utters an odd sound and thereafter few of the pack begin to creep around the house.

Aware that these critters, powerful as they are, do not fit through the windows, Tendjan forthwith commands that everyone draw a sword.

Throwing over a table, he says, "They can only come in through front door! I say, hear me: Stand behind this table and thrust when they are near!"

And the door falls thereupon, and the beast beyond the threshold unveils with slobbering maw, gnashing its teeth at their sight, though keeping its ground; and one of the other beasts yet creeping about, lunges at a window, causing all but Tendjan to see whether it could enter.

"LOOK TO THE FORE!" he shouts at his fellows, seeing the beast ahead charging at them.

Ramming the table, driving back its prey, the beast forces them nearer to the window, through which one of the others snatches Tendjan. Diving in with its head, straight sinking its teeth into his neck, the beast tears him out into open field and slashes the skin off his face, cutting apart the muscle beneath, shredding his eyes, and tearing off his lower jaw—all done by a single strike.

NEARBY: Arianna, ever so quick on her feet, is trying to escape the beasts' assails, not once thinking about Tendjan or the others she was with. Whatever may happen to them, she cares not and runs to the stable to mount a horse.

The never ending begs for help are ever so clear; and the creatures' rumbling roars and growls, each of their yelps and howls, shiver her down to her every bone, startling her, driving her into terror, letting her run on the verge of panic. Every wail of pain, anguish and dismay shatters all her courage, burying it beneath the desire to get away. Darting into the stable, she grabs the first saddle she sees, thereupon realizing the small stream of blood beneath her feet. It takes no longer than an instant 'til she awakes to the horses' escape, one of which must have been injured. And she curses them and begins to cry, throwing the saddle away.

"I hate you, Artias!" says she. "I will have you killed!"

Her threats seem hollow, spoken out of desperation, and no tear she sheds for those who died or yet will. All she sees is her end, for she knows she cannot make off on foot—this night, it might claim her life. She nevertheless summons her courage and tries her utmost to survive, panic-stricken rubbing her skin with horse dung to take her smell; and she covers herself in straw, caring little about her father, who strives to get into the tavern, which front door has been barred and any other way in barricaded.

"OPEN THE DOOR!" Unelas orders the guards he sent into the tavern. "I SAY, OPEN IT NOW!"

From beyond, he can hear every voice of every soul he wished to feed off saying that his guards are no more.

"These vile men sought to aid their own," say the people, "caring about none of us! They are surely dead by now, and you will have joined them at sunrise!"

Unelas strikes at the door, kicks and spits at it, and yet he never stops begging the people behind to let him in, yelling then, "HOW DARE YOU, HOW DARE YOU LEAVE YOUR ELDER TO DIE!"

"I promised you!" He hears Artias' voice among the screams and turns to face him with drawn blade, unable to say a mere word when the hunter disarms him and straight forces the sword all through his body; and he thereupon, with one swing at the Elder's neck, cuts his head straight off.

Banging the pommel against the tavern's front door, Artias demands whichever guards he assumes to be inside to open up.

"Unelas is dead, and if you not wish to die too, then do open this door forthwith!"

The people in the tavern are aware of the peril outside and let him in without delay, whereupon Artias slams close the door and speaks into the group, "Come forth now, you ill guards!"

"They are gone," says a lean fellow with shaking knees.

Having secured the front door with the bar, he quickly turns to Artias, telling him that the guards left to help the others. "But they weren't allowed in anymore thereon," says he. "We left them to die, cared not to hear their cries, but what else should we have done—they would have killed us!"

Nodding shortly, Artias lays a hand upon the man's shoulder.

"You need not feel guilty; they have brought their deaths upon themselves."

In sight of every frightened soul he is among, Artias advises them to be quiet; and he then treads carefully to Faron (the barman), asking him where he stores his wine.

"In, in the cellar," says Faron in a whisper.

"Get me all you have. Quick now!"

Telling the people that they must not be afraid, for the beasts certainly have enough fare, Artias sets about checking if there are any other ways in, saying, "I will secure the area quickly"; yet the people say, "We have already made sure that there is no way in anymore."

"We have barricaded everything," say they, never speaking much louder than a whisper. "But now we have nothing left to barricade the door."

"You mustn't barricade it. Not only would it cause too much noise, you would also begin to sweat. The beasts shall not hear nor smell you. Say, did you close the shutters, too?"

"No," says Alarion, holding an iron pan as a weapon. "the guards, they did that after they forced us to hush."

"I must check everything again nevertheless. Please, do not leave each other alone. The beasts have already claimed enough prey for a night, but we must not take risks."

"I can hear them," says a young man, clutching his beloved's hand. "I can hear them growling and, and—what if they are aware of us?"

"You must be still." At all times Artias speaks calmly, never anxiously. "I say, no harm will come to you."

"We could die!" says the boy, shocking his dearest; and she lays her head upon his chest, begging him to be still and embrace her.

"Please hold me near," says she. "I do not want to die!"

But a word spoken in distress rises everyone's fear of death; and they all, from the youngest to the oldest, lay their fate in Artias' hands, seeking his leadership.

"Do not let us be taken," they beg of him; "and please, oh, please do ward us," they say to him; "and be our shield," they proceed.

At each growl they shriek with fear, snivel, tremble at the thought of the jaws they could find themselves in. Holding near their children, whispering that Artias is here and that he will protect them, for he is their shield, they unintentionally propel him into taking the obligations of an Elder.

"Shall we go down to the cellar?" they ask him. "The basement is underground—beasts will not dig through to us, or?"

"No. There is no way to escape from the cellar. We will be trapped if attacked. Just stay here and be still."

Parting from them, Artias walks warily from room to room, proud of the people every time he sees how well they have used whatever furniture around to seal themselves in.

Upon returning to them, he espies a box of wine on the bar.

"That is all I have," says Faron. "However, I must show you something, Artias—I really have to show you something."

"What is—"

"I better show you, not tell you."

Nodding shortly, Artias turns to the people, commanding them to "Take a bottle of wine. You must all take a bottle and pour the wine over you to take your smell—do so thoroughly, drench yourself to have no beast whiff you."

"Show me now," he then says to Faron, following him down to the basement, where, at very first, Artias smells an awkward odor.

"What has happened here?"

"You remember"—Faron looks up at the celling, hearing the others following Artias' command—"the guy your friend killed. Unelas, he let the body be brought down here and had it besprinkled with salt. He said he will bury the body the next day, but I found my cellar clean, no body."

With worries looking over the floor, Artias sees merely dust and dirt, no hatch, no fireplace, nothing that seems like an entrance to another feasting chamber. And on wandering his eyes from every barrel and shelve to each moldering board and solid beam, he wonders, "What could he have done with it here? There is not much space, but it must be here. I can sm—"

"No, I, I know where it is, for I found it."

"Where?"

Faron nods at a barrel, a barrel tall enough to reach to his belly. A terrifying thought comes upon Artias; and he, only slowly steps to the barrel.

"Have you opened it?"

"Yes, well, I closed it again very quickly, I can tell you!"

"Listen to me carefully, Faron, keep this to yourself."

"Yes, of course, but what about the body? The beasts might smell it."

"Leave it here for the night. We cannot bring it away now."

"But what about the beasts, Artias?"

"They should have enough to eat outside. However, I—"

"We could throw it out of a window."

"I will have no window opened, no barricade removed—leave it here. At sunrise we shall burry him."

"As you say."

"Come."

"Tell me, just why would he keep this here for so long, risking someone to find it? Maybe there are other bodies!"

"As I see it, he simply forgot—" In an instant Artias falls silent.

"What?" utters Faron.

"Explain to me: Why have you not smelled it before! Can it be—and I am choosing my words carefully, Faron—that you knew of it, of this body."

"Hold your tongue there, what are you accusing me of? I am hardly ever down here! I keep my stock in the rooms above, not here. There are rats here, more than upstairs—they used to eat through my supplies. If you do not believe me, take a look at the barrel. The rats have already eaten through it. They were gnawing at the body when I risked to look into that barrel."

"You fetched the wine from down here."

"What? That was the reserve—I always keep one box of wine in reserve."

Artias says nothing, though his eyes say enough.

"I did not do anything!"

Straight returning upstairs, Artias heads behind the bar and rummages around for an iron plate, bowl, or pan. Having found one in Alarion's grasp, he asks him to hand it over. "I need that pan."

"But I have it to defend my wife."

"Hand it to him!" says his wife, driven by her desperation. "He needs it, so let him have it!"

"Okay, okay—here, take it."

Confused, Alarion observes Artias making a small fire in it.

"For what is that?" he asks.

"I need smoke."

Faron joins them then, anxiously asking Artias if he still trusts him.

"Why are you asking me this?"

Glancing at the people, Faron sees their glares and rather not say a word more.

"You must be quiet," says an old man with a staff. "Artias told us to be quiet, so you be quiet now—everybody be quiet now!"

Though all Faron wished was to assert that he took no part in Unelas' doings, he merely says to Artias, "I would die for my fellowmen."

"I believe you," says Artias and descents to the basement again, laying the pan upon the barrel. Hoping that whichever beast around will smell smoke well above the odor of fouling flesh, he returns to the people, asking them to show patience now and stay silent.

And the people, all drenched with wine, hush and hug around their loved ones; and they look at the hunter, feeling shielded and grateful to have him in their midst.

Though doing his utmost to keep everyone safe, Artias doubts he can ward them through this night anytime he hears the beasts lurking about beyond the tavern's walls. They are heard growling, howling and yelping 'til finally silence descends.

When the beasts seem to be gone, Artias does not move; he is wise enough to wait for a while longer.

"Artias," says Faron, "Artias, please, I must speak to you."

The people feel nervous, begin to wonder why Faron is taking Artias away from them always and always again.

"What do you want of him?" says the old man, raising his staff at Faron. "What is it with you!"

"I need to talk to him!"

"About what?"

"I was the one who took the beating for you, so do not—"

"Enough!" Artias strikes in. "Put down your staff straight; and you, Faron, what beating are you speaking of?"

"Ask this old man here. He knows what I speak of—ungrateful geezer."

"They would have killed him," says a hale fellow. "He raised his staff at the guards, too, shouting at them, saying they are traitors, 'til he was brought to silence with fists. Faron took the beating for him, and he barricaded the door when the guards left—he and Alarion did."

"Is that true?" Artias inquires of Alarion, who nods and claps Faron on the back.

"Thank you," says Artias to this brave barman. "I believe you are a brave man, Faron. Forgive me for—"

"No, you are the brave one here. If it weren't for you, we might be dead by now. You are our shield. You ward us and guide us, and you keep us safe and sheltered."

Artias rises, telling everyone apart from Faron to stay where they are at.

"We are we going?" wonders the barman.

"I will risk and look around outside. I will go out through a window, a window which shutters you must close once I have left."

"You will be eaten if you go out!"

"Do not fear. Now, listen here, I will knock on the front door as soon as you are safe to leave your shelter. Until then, stay here, calm and still."

Carefully, vigilantly at all times, Artias climbs out of the window and signs Faron to close the shutter right away.

Parts of the tavern's walls are stained with blood, and there lies a limb just a step ahead of him; and this leg, with the bone arising beneath ripped flesh, seems to have been torn off the body.

Whilst heading towards the heart of Veran, trails of blood fall into his sight; and he finds torches dying out in the blood of the fallen and many weapons, from bows to swords, among pieces of shredded clothes and flesh. And on treading cautiously along the path to the center, he discovers houses with bloody floors and breached doors, yet he descries not a single body anywhere. Whether the pack has already withdrawn into the forest is yet to be seen. Until now, though, he neither sees nor hears them—they seem to be gone.

The only steps that reach his hearing sound not like the tread of a beast but a person. Forthwith tracing the footfall in hopes of finding his fellow Janderas alive and well (although he saw him die by the claws of a beast), he is consumed by ire upon seeing who is seeking shelter. Careless of any beasts still around, he cries, "ARIANNA!"

Promptly quickening her pace, her only drive is to outrun him, for she knows he will slay her.

"I will have you killed," yells she—and with an arrow in her leg she falls on the bloody ground, screaming to feel the arrowhead deep within her thigh; and there before her, against all that Artias expects, emerges his fellow Janderas with a fine bow in firm grasp.

"The beast that came upon me," he says to Arianna, "I will show you now how that felt like!"

"You and the lots of you are all the same"—she holds her leg, feels the blood running—"no exceptions. Where is Tendjan. TENDJAN!"

"Where do you think he is, you witch!"

"He will kill y—"

"HE IS DEAD!" Janderas shouts. "I saw how they snatched him—wearing fell won't trick the claws of the forest!"

"I should have told him to bring you to the hole so that you would be among the others who lie buried under my father's house! In the feasting cambers your bodies should rot. Bone among bone! And you, Artias, you will be dealt with. I will call every bandit tribe together and send them after you!"

Artias comes to his friend, looking down on the woman who acted so spitefully and wicked.

"Beheaded be my foe and dreaded my name," Janderas says to his fellow. "Make it quick."

"I dare you, Artias!" utters Arianna, knowing very well what should happened now. "I will have my veng—"

And through her neck he strikes, cutting off her head.

"*All (be) by**" says Janderas thereupon. "Bone among bone."

However much Artias would like to embrace his fellow, Janderas is suffering from a wound which must be attended to at once, for the claws of some beasts are often dirty and smeared with the blood of their prey, causing deadly infections.

"Quick!" he says. "Come with me."

"There is no need to rush."

"I see your wound, right there beneath your torn armor—across your chest, you bleed all across your chest."

Swaying slightly, Janderas says that he managed to walk here, even could fire an arrow.

"A clean shot," says he, then and there dropping on the ground.

What was, is and will be
What he was asked for in the end he would have never expected, and he would have never thought to be given the respect, love and trust of all the souls who look up to him.

Hoisting Janderas onto his shoulder, Artias hurries to the tavern, wary at all times lest he be set upon.

"Open up!" cries he, standing before the tavern.

The first to emerge from beyond the door is a woman whose face turns pale at the sight of the blood dripping down the hunter's chest; and she gawks at the lifeless man he is bearing, asking if he is dead.

"He needs a healer!" utters Artias anxiously, stepping into the tavern. "Who of you knows how to treat a wounded man? He must be attended to urgently!"

"Let me see," says a man, a man whom Artias would have never thought of as a healer.

"Alarion, you know the art of healing?"

The blood running from Janderas' wound over the hunter's shoulder and chest alarms Alarion; the wound must be bad, a gash, deep and demanding his very best to clean and seal.

"Is this from a beast's claw?" asks he.

"Yes. The wound must be cleaned, washed thoroughly—Alarion, you must rid the risk of an infection."

"Quick, lay him on a table!"

"No, follow me to my room," says Faron, grabbing a small candle and straight escorting them to the only storeroom in the tavern used for resting. His only dwelling, bare and clean, is stained with blood upon their arrival.

Fetching two candles from a small shelf by the door, he places them together on a stool, which he shoves over to the bed, and thereupon lights the candles.

"Put him on the bed," says Alarion to Artias, astonishingly clear in his speech. "I need thread and needle, Faron, thread and needle, water, a towel, and... herbs—the herbs are in my house."

"Where is your house?" asks Artias, laying Janderas on the bed.

"Right—no, wait—left, go left when you step out of the tavern. I always hang my belt on a hook on the door—I need my belt, Artias."

"I will fetch it."

"Wait," utters Faron, handing him the candle he is bearing; "you will be needing this."

Artias nods in gratitude and leaves at once. Straight heading for Alarion's house, he soon stands before a shredded door, passing through the threshold into bloody ground. In the middle of the chaos searching for the belt, he rummages through shards of wood, though finding merely the hook.

He arises, roaming the floor with his eyes, trying to espy the belt; and he looks under the stand by the door, at last discovering the belt under a nearby chair.

Alarion has already laid bare Janderas' chest and set about cleaning the gash as Artias returns and forthwith hands him the belt.

"An awful wound," says Alarion, digging out a plant with a brush-like flower from a leather pouch tied to his belt, "but fear not, it is not as sever as you may think—fortune smiled upon him; if Janderas hand't worn armor, he would have died. His chest muscles, strong as they are, might have reduced the penetration of the claws, yet the armor saved his life."

With gentle pressure Alarion squeezes some of the plant's juice into a bowl with water, thereupon soaking the flower in it.

"It is not large enough," mutters he, dropping the entire flower into the water, which viscous juice begins to collect at the surface of the water. "I need the towel — Faron, where is the towel?"

"Here," utters Faron, showing Alarion all the rags and towels he fetched.

Alarion carefully remove's the plant's flower, wraps it in the towel and holds it into the water. Having drenched the towel, he squeezes out the water over Janderas' wound before rubbing around the gash, cleaning the injured skin.

Looking at Faron in between of watching Alarion going about his trade, Artias says to him, "Faron, could you please return to the others and make sure they stay calm."

"All right. You just call me if you need anything."

"Thank you, I will — oh, and, Faron, tell them I will be with them shortly."

"I will."

"Thank you," says Artias, forth on observing Alarion, who says that the flower he used has the ability to disinfect a wound but can cause itchiness.

"For how long?"

"For about a day. Certain wounds to living tissue itch during healing, but not as much as his will — of course, that is because of the flower."

"I will tell him."

"No, don't! There are certain characters who have a tendency to feel — how shall I say. Once you tell them their wound could start to itch, they will immediately feel it, out of nowhere, just so, even if it hasn't begun to itch yet."

"I understand. I will not tell him, then."

"You can when he begins to scratch, because he should not scratch too fiercely."

Sometime later Janderas twitches and not long after awakens, drawing a breath at very first.

"How do you feel?" asks Alarion, inspecting Janderas state of mind.

"Wounded."

Utterly relieved, Artias steps closer to the bend, smiling his joy as his fellow says, "That was quite an experience—was I gone long?"

"It is still night, not even dawning yet."

"I see."

"Okay"—Alarion holds thread and needle ready to stitch, showing both to Janderas —"this is going to feel... not so nice." And then he begins stitching the wound, with skill handling needle and thread.

To see how versed Alarion is in the art of healing lets Artias realize how greatly Unelas had misled him—he could have very well helped Gordes (recover from his long, laborious march), if only he had wanted to: summoning Alarion would have been all it needed.

Bearing the pain, however great, Janderas says that Gordes did not deserve to die such an awful death.

"In sight of the woman he loved he passed away. I say, we should bury him!"

"His body is gone, Janderas. They are all gone."

"I must say, knowing that a critter ate him gives me some comfort."

"Really?"

"Yes, well—give me a moment quickly."

"Bear with me," says Alarion, carefully stitching his way along the wound.

"It needs more than"—squeezing close his eyes, for the pain is truly vicious, Janderas holds his breath, waiting for the needled to leave his flesh—"just some creature to kill me."

"Well, good armor is always an advantage," says Artias.

"Good armor helps no blind man! And O how blind we were, Artias. We did not see, we did not see through her lies, her play—hers and her father's."

"Do not anger yourself."

"You know what"—gashing his teeth at the throbbing pain of his wound, he hushes for an instant—"what she said to me? She said we should have been brou—"

"I was there. I heard what she said."

"That wicked—"

"Listen, Janderas, I must go see the people. Just stay here an—"

"Good shot, wasn't it?"

"What?"

"The arrow, her leg—I say I took a well aim for someone who isn't an archer."

"Janderas, you should not speak but rest. I will come to see you shortly, all right?"

Artias leaves to speak to the others then.

Seeing how everybody looks at him as he emerges, he asks them to be patient for a moment longer.

"I will be with you shortly," he promises them, saying then that he must risk a look outside to make sure no beast returned.

Glimpses through one of the shutters, he beholds the moon shining down upon reeded ground. In sight of the houses, their wrecked doors and bloody floors, he wonders how to back the people of this place, how to guide and help them find a place where they will not fall prey to the wicked again, and he then turns to them, asking them to come around, for "I have something to say."

"Is your friend, all right?" a woman asks, thereupon saying that she did not think of him as the brave man he is before this very night. "I wish to apologize to him."

"He must rest for now, my dear." Looking at everyone around him, he continues, "I ask you, people of Veran, do you wish to stay here, or do you want to join me and my kin in the northern plan?"

"The northern plain is far away," says Faron. "We might die before even reaching it."

"If you decide to stay here, then we must clean every house and turn the earth around. Every bit of flesh must be dug in, and guards must be chosen and an Elder declared."

"How shall we turn the earth around?" wonders Faron.

"With shovels we will raise the soil and put it down the other way around. Maybe we are lucky and blessed with rain overnight. We must not worry about the bloody earth, then."

"I do not think that we will have any rain in the coming days."

"That is yet to be seen. Right now there is nothing we can do anyway. You all must stay here in the tavern 'til dawn. Select guards and thinking about whom you wish to have as your Elder."

There is a hefty man with great hands who steps out of the crowd, with a nod pointing at Artias. "I say, you shall be our Elder."

Every soul agrees, saying to Artias that he alone shall be declared Elder of Veran; and they ask him if that would be to his pleasing.

"Because you have saved us all, we cannot think of any other leader," say the people, and then continue with deep affection, "We all vow to follow your advice and obey to your rules, and whomever you want to be a guard will be a guard, and whomever you want to be your penman will—"

"Enough," utters Artias. "I will tell you at dawn, but until then, make sure you find rest, and stay together."

"Will the beasts return?" ask the people, approaching him as if he already agreed to be their Elder.

"They might, but I doubt they will. Just stay in the tavern close by the fireplace, rest around the hearth. You will be seeing the Sun's rays shining through the shutters soon."

With this said Artias leaves them alone again and returns to his fellow.

Alarion, whose healing skills are even beyond Artias' hopes, comes to him, saying, "Your friend is sleeping now."

"I thank you for your aid. I believe you are a great healer."

"Your friend, a strong man he is. I bandaged up his wound and gave him something to ease his suffering. He will not be needing anything else than rest now—oh, and I should warn you, he may act differently than before."

"Why so?"

"There is a certain plant which eases pain and relaxes one's mind. Some people act quite oddly when given this plant."

"Oddly meaning what exactly?"

"Well, have you ever seen a drunken man?"

"I have seen many in my life, Alarion."

"Well, he will be much worse. Should the plant have an effect on him, that is. But it, it is not like he will be violent or so, simply—well—oddly; or very, very tired."

"Thank you for telling me."

"I am with the others, so I am close by should anything arise. I shall see you later, Artias."

Nodding gratefully Artias wishes him a good night's rest, saying then that he must not fear to rest, for the beasts have withdrawn into the forest by now. "However, do stay in the tavern."

Trying to be silent (for he does not wish to rouse Janderas), Artias enters the room and sits on the floor beside the bed, leaning against the wall while thinking about the people's request. These people need an Elder; if there is no one they can turn to, then how likely is it that they will have a disagreement over the best course of actions if ever they find themselves in such a peril as tonight again. They will be depending on a show of hands then, in which case there could be some who tell their fellows when to raise their hands; and if ever they have no time to decide, then who will be there to guide them. To him, the best for the people here or in any other village is to have a leader who is mindful of the dangers of his decisions, attentive to his peoples' needs and interests, tolerant and patience; and, above all, eager to better the future. He must be brave, willing to rank his needs below that of his people. If he agrees to be such a man, then there will be no ventures forth on, and he must be ready to take the blame should ever his decisions lead to misfortune. But he is not sure if he can give them this just yet and tries to part from his thoughts, soon finding himself pondering over his foes' actions.

He assumes, after many troublesome thoughts, that Unelas' guards could have been those whom Arianna wanted to met in the forest. It might be that she had her father's dagger with her to let them know whose daughter she is. She surely knew the way to Veran but needed protection on her way there. However, she is not the only one whose actions prey on his mind.

Each member of the tribe Janderas and his kin had set upon were related to Tendjan, either by blood or fellowship. Given what Unelas said, Artias assumes that Tendjan was in Odas, backed by a small group, during the attack on his kith and kin. Neither Tendjan nor any one of his fellows could have known what happened 'til they had returned to the cave, finding their own slain. They might have departed for Veran thereupon to see their leader and arrived while he (Artias) was speaking to Arianna. Unelas most likely was the head of the tribe and told Tendjan that the hunter and Janderas are in Veran yet again and that it's time to act before they cause more trouble.

Unfortunately, however it might have been, the actually truth Artias can only guess at; there is no way of knowing what exactly happened. He merely knows, without doubt, that his deeds and doings forced every one of them to change their course of actions more than once.

"Your sister will shout at me." He hears his fellow saying.

Seeing Janderas awake and seemingly well, he smiles, though advises him to rest nevertheless.

"I pass out and awake again, and then I pass out and awake again."

"How are you feeling?"

"Tired. Yes, just tired—oh, I am so very tired."

"I thought you died. If I had known you were alive, I wouldn't have—"

"Hush. I though I am dead myself. Until I saw I had actually slain the beast, I lay on the ground, wondering what might come. You now how that feels like, to suddenly discover that you are not dead?"

"I can't say I do."

"As if you were wasting time, that's how it feels like. Anyway, good you killed that woman, Artias—for a moment I thought you would not."

"Say, Tendjan is dead, right? I mean, you did see his body, right?"

"I saw him being taken."

"Maybe he is alive."

"*Let it all be thrown into one grave**, Artias!" Quietly Janderas looks at the celling, then he begins to gawk at his hands, saying to Artias, "Perhaps you can help me solve a mystery?"

"A mystery?"

"Yes, a mystery."

"All right, say, what puzzles you?"

"Did you ever ask yourself why we need five fingers on one hand, although we would be well off with four? I do assume we have five because there was no space for a sixth one."

"Who's to say, my fellow."

"Did you know that there are places where women are accused of being a witch when they give birth to a crippled son. Even when just one finger is crippled, they are brought to the stake. It is said that witches bear a grudge against men, trying to extinct them by brining forth crippled sons only. Please, promise me, Artias, promise me to watch out for my wife. She shall never face such wrong!"

"Not ever shall such wickedness find its way into Arjovan. And if I must take up arms against a host of men, I will to perish those foul in heart."

"Greed, Artias, greed gives rises to evil, and where there is evil, there is wrong! Just think of Unelas, Arianna, whoever else, not you nor me were onto their play. We fell prey. As we have, so will others in the days to come—when I think of this land's future, I am filled with foreboding."

"I do feel the same."

E 0.6

Their deeds were righteous and their doings for the best of every soul upon Earth. They acted bravely and faced what came with courage and sword; they stood steadfast, did not yield in sight of the odds, did not waver when came upon, and though it is that their names are no more in our thoughts, we thank them with all our hearts.

Many months have past since Artias decided to become the Elder of Veran. He first of all declared that the stockade be built finish and that a town hall and two watchtowers come to be, and he made sure that his guards learn how to fight and that they have a day and night shift, and he let them be equipped with shields, swords, and bows and commanded that they dress alike in proper armor; and he said they shall broaden their knowledge of beasts and herbs and develop an understanding of the creatures' realm.

Because he cares for his people, always making sure that they have all they need and sometimes even withdraws into his house to continue writing down a law or draw a map, he is held in heigh regard for his achievements. To this day, he is deemed a great Elder.

Janderas has fully recovered, merely bearing a scar across his chest which should always remind him of the fortune of having survived the attack. He has returned to Delmar long ago, telling his wife of his venture with her brother and divulging to her the ordeal of his life.

Whenever he can withdraw from his strive for justice for a spell, he travels to Veran alone or with Artias' kin, smiling at the thought of seeing his fellow again; and Artias himself is filled with joy, always thrilled when his guards tell him that his kin have come; and whenever they sit together, talking of everything and nothing, he says to them that he thought about changing the village name but has not been blessed with an idea yet, until Tanara suggests that the village be named after the word for sanctuary in Nahess, Idorra. Recently it has been given this name.

PRESENTLY: The day has yet dawned when Artias sits at a table together with a man who claims himself a mapmaker. Erios, as this man's name is, has arrived at Idorra sometime ago, making known to the guards and the people that he is a drawer of maps and would like to know whether they can tell him of specific locations. Shortly after he was summoned by Artias.

"Many days I spend in the open, marking everything I come across," he tells Artias. "But say, why did you wish to see me?"

"Well"—Artias rises from his chair and fetches the map he draws—"my guards told me of your trade, so I thought you might be able to help me complete this map."

"Fine guards you have. No others ever asked me to state my reasons for a visit. Makes you feel safe once inside, especially nowadays. Anyway, what do you wish?"

"What do you mean by 'nowadays'? Is there trouble?"

"Well, at times, you find yourself among doubtful characters. Did you know that once upon a time people ate each other?"

"That wasn't very long ago."

"No?"

"In this village dwelled the most wicked souls."

"I have heard people speaking of a hunter who not only helped those in need but also saved the people of an entire village—perhaps they spoke of Idorra."

"Where did you hear that from?"

"In Delmar that was. At times I find myself writing stories, and a man in Delmar said I should write about this hunter and the good-hearted men at his side."

—FUTURE: Though the mapmaker will have written down the hunter's venture in the years to come and even display the story in part on wooden tablets along the main roads made in E0.1, neither Artias nor his ever so brave companions will be known of in the years to come after their passing. Many heroes will be born in Arjovan, and as many will be forgotten in time. There are but a few whose names will continue to exist in the hearts and minds of the people, and there will be some whose names will be honored and others whose names will be feared, and though among all these there is the one whose name will never be forgotten, for his deeds will never grow forgotten, every soul who has fought and still will fight to better the future 'til to the day of the greatest change in the land have allowed all that is to come to be. Their names may vanish out of the people's thoughts and their deeds may not be passed on, but their achievements endure throughout all the *Eras** of the land and beyond.

GLOSSARY

All (be) by
said when either a pleasant or unpleasant experience is or seems to be over.

Beheaded be my foe and dreaded my name
being strong enough to kill one's enemy and have others fear one's name as a result of this.

Day's first light
Dawn

Day's last light
Dusk

Eastern forest
When Armora (the first city in the history of Arjovan) is built in E0.1, the region wherein the eastern forest lies is given the name *Reogan*, meaning 'earliest' in Nahess.

Eastern mountain
This mountain will be given the name *Anheran Camveral*, meaning 'The Holly's rock to descend' in Nahess. Later on, however, it will be known as *Camveral* only.

Eras
Eras refer to specific events in the history of Arjovan one of which is the discovery of the land in E0.10.

ERAS NE: Dawn of Arjovan
ERAS NA: Raise of Armora

ERAS NO: Fellenveil
ERAS NU: Rise of man
ERAS NOB: Harganos' sword
ERAS NAL: Garhos Jaro
ERAS NAD: Vengarth rage
ERAS NIO: Neerdos' perish
ERAS NEES: Ferja's death
ERAS NAR: Eronomus' birth

Eras 'historical event': origin unknown, though assumed to be an abbreviation of the phrase, *Het-he-de ahres Rohn ües geädet hat*, 'this which event in history has changed us'; which is originated from *Enähr neh arth Rohn de ostarck arey Saen*, 'Savage be an event which strongly impinged on life'—has been used in literary since well around E0.9.
Ne, Na, No, etc., are notations that will be first used in E40.10 to identify the single Eras no more by name only.

Kandus
One of the three major trees (Giagonus, Kandus, Jantarus) up to 200 feet (60meters) in height that grows most commonly in the land, with an enormous trunk and a great crown.

Let it all be throw into one grave
used to indicate that there is no sense in discussing a particular subject, especially an unpleasant or disturbing one.

Nahess
This language is only spoken by the wandering tribes who had discovered the new land and named it after the word for Sun, Arjovan. Since

people from other lands had been invited to live in Arjovan, English replaced Nahess almost entirely. These days, it is rarely heard, but certain names such as Odas (home) are Nahess in origin. See below.

Ardegan
from *ardä*, 'keen', and *Gan*, 'eye'; a man with keen eyesight.

Artias
from *art*, 'a', and *Ias*, 'giver'; a-giver (of something helpful such as advice).

Beras
from *Erios*, 'storyteller'.

Giagonus
from *Giagonto*, 'giant'.

Gilgaron
from *gil*, 'run', and *garona*, 'quick'; a quick runner; sprinter.

Tarion
from *taorina*, 'witted'; a smart man.

Tindras
from *tind*, 'quiet', and *Ras*, 'man'; a quiet man.

Idorra
'sanctuary', thought to be from a phrase meaning 'so be in refuge.'

Jantarus
'emperor'

Kandus
from *Kandal*, 'bulwark', and the noun *dus*, 'wood', as adjective, *dus* (after the noun): 'wooden bulwark'.

Northern plain
In the years to come, a traveler will discover that this plain is not as large as formerly assumed and that it lies to the northeast in relation to the mountains. This discovery will arise issues as to the correctness of maps. From then on, all previously drawn maps will be deemed to be incorrect and the plain will be named *Grän Falde* 'Green field'. Much later, however, it will be renamed Ahron, after a mighty swordsman, who will bring many soldiers to the sword during Fellenveil, the religious war more than two hundred years after the discovery of the land.

Sky's falls
A cloudburst, especially one following a drought.

Southern forest
While Armora is being raised, mapmakers are commanded to characterize geographical features of the entire land. They will name this forest *Naturas Rochgara* for its flora, meaning 'Nature's fruitful garden'; but there will be a debate on whether or no *Naturas Rochgara* could be confused for the name of a plant. Eventually, it will be marked and referred to as *Rochgar* only; however, as the 'a' in *Rochgara* is omitted, the name will be reviewed as incorrect by linguists, unless an apostrophe is used to indicate the omission of the letter. In the years to follow, *Rochgar* will stand for a region and will be therefore, despite the the omission of the 'a', be regarded as correct.

Sun's grace (also **Sun's 'brace**)
Sunlight, especially when regarded as healthy.

The creatures' realm (also **the realm of beast**)
Any area of ground or region uninhabited or sparsely inhabited by Man; the wilds and wilderness.

ORIGIN: This way of referring to the wilds was first introduced by Artias during a conversation with fishermen who spoke of the seas as "the first kingdom". Having nothing better to say, Artias referred to the wilderness as the creatures' realm. Later on, the meat-eating creatures of the wilds will be referred to as "the claws of the forest".

The divine being
Over four hundred years after Artias' ventures, the being he though to be divine will emerge in legions and be deemed the greatest peril yet to walk the land.

Western mountain
The western mountain will later on be named *Gordonial* by a mapmaker, meaning 'Blizzard Rock'. The name relates to the weather on the mountain in winter.
Originally it will have been meant to be named *Storma of Freeze ol starck Onial*, meaning 'Sever winter storms upon strong rock'; however, this will be regarded as inappropriate for a map.